The Tiger of Canton

by G. H. Teed

Cover illustration from the original by Eric Parker

From No, 623 (New Series).—Sexton Blake Library, dated June 1938. First published in the Sexton Blake Library, New Series, April 1927.

Stillwoods Edition 2019

GHTeed.Blogspot.Com

Catalogue information:
Title: The Tiger of Canton
Author: G. H. Teed (1886-1938)
From No, 623 (New Series).—SEXTON BLAKE LIBRARY, dated June 1938. First published in the Sexton Blake Library, New Series, April 1927.
This Edition: Stillwoods, 2019.
ISBN Canada: 978-1-988304-65-6
Author Blog: GHTeed.Blogspot.Com
Blog: Stillwoods.Blogspot.Ca
Storefront: http://www.lulu.com/spotlight/lulubook22

Cover Image adapted from original illustration
From the magazine:
THE LEADING DETECTIVE-STORY MAGAZINE. Four New Volumes appear on the first Thursday of next month. Order them NOW!

A thrilling story of adventure in Northern Africa, Paris and London. Featuring SEXTON BLAKE'S old and dangerous enemy GEORGE MARSDEN PLUMMER and his equally fearless companion VALI MATA-VALI.

Introduction:
The interest in Sexton Blake stories began in 1893! Author G. H. Teed's first recognized Blake story was in 1910 with The Mystery of Room 11.

Teed like his fictional hero Sexton Blake was a world traveller. Teed was born in New Brunswick, Canada, but after graduating university he wanted to see palm trees so he started his travels with the Caribbean. He worked his way eventually to Australia, and his trip to England began the launch of his writing career.

At some time he decided a trip to the orient was necessary. This trip was even reported upon in the Sexton Blake editorials of the time!

The Tiger of Canton is an interesting relation of people, places, customs and crime. "If a case could not be solved, Sexton Blake was the man to solve it—" From 1927, originally, comes this story; it is unusual in that our villain commits three murders, and the story touches four continents!

CHAPTER 1. The Great Pilgrimage—George Marsden Plummer Patiently Waits to Plunge Into Some New Plot.

FOR three weeks a hundred thousand pilgrims had been converging on Meknes from every corner of Northern Africa. For it is at Meknes that the great fanatical commemoration of the Prophet's birthday takes place towards the end of the month of September.

Meknes is little known to the infidel, but to the Moslem world it stands a sacred place of pilgrimage little less to be regarded than Mecca. It is a beautiful and wonderful old place lying on the northern slopes of the Middle Atlas Mountains, in Morocco, not far distant from Fez, that hotbed of intrigue from which nine-tenths of the mischief in Morocco has emanated.

But where Fez is bustling and eager and greedy, Meknes is an indolent beauty, living almost entirely in the glory of a past greatness, and waking up only once a year when the feast of Mulud is celebrated. It is there that is situated the famous mosque of Sidi ben Aissa, comparatively modern as regards the town itself, or the ancient Roman ruins of Volubilis which lie close at hand. But it is the canonising of the founder of this fanatical sect— the Aissawa—that has given rise to the annual pilgrimage.

On the occasion with which this record deals, the number of pilgrims was greater than ever. From every point of the compass they had been coming for days and weeks, and as each group straggled in they pitched their bivouac in the first available spot, some within the city walls, some immediately without, getting as close to the sacred mosque of Sidi ben Aissa as possible, and later comers in the bare valleys and gorges of the surrounding hills. And, towering over all, the mighty grandeur of the Jebel-el-Thelj, or Snowy Mountains.

Endless the procession seemed to be. Came wealthy Moslems, mounted and attended by well-horsed bodyguards; came more modest processions on foot; came straggling parties of beggars in rags. Everywhere was a vast, low-hanging cloud of dust stirred up by the padding, scraping, shuffling footsteps of camels and horses and men. Women rode behind their lords or shared a palfrey; others, less favoured, trudged up the burning slopes with babies slung on their backs, and older children stumbling along wearily.

To be remarked among the hordes were the savage Berbers from the fertile, wooded hills beyond Azru; light-tinted men from Fez, dressed in snowy white burnouses, prosperous and silky of manner; stern-faced men from the sandy wastes of Algeria and Tunisia and Tripoli; flat-nosed negroids from the south of the mountains; women of the Ouled Nails with the blue tribal mark on the forehead; a vast, seething multitude gathered from the fecundity of that little-known country of the Moor come together for this one purpose—to celebrate in repulsive abandon the feast of the Prophet.

Among those who found accommodation within the city were the rich merchants from Fez and Algiers. These would transact certain business while there, for all around Meknes are prolific olive groves. But not until the great feast of Mulud was over would the traders of Meknes descend to business. Until then the place was a vast patch of moving colour, of dust and constant crescendo, and of every smell under the sun.

On the "day of days" the tumult and confusion reached its zenith. From the moment that dawn spread pink across a cloudless sky the fanatics, whose devotion to Aissawa had brought them there, prepared for the great orgy which would last the whole day and culminate in a frenzy of animal abandon at night. Stripped to the waist, hair flying loose, or else polls shaved close, they gathered in mobs, beginning the working up of their passions by jumping and dancing and shouting to the steady beat of tomtoms and the harsh crashing of cymbals.

All through the morning they kept this up, while the crowds who had come to watch grew denser and denser, being kept away from the active participators only by the efforts of horsed attendants.

By midday the scene was one of appalling sweat and shrieking clamour. Nor fatigue nor pause did those dancing fanatics know. Whirling and prancing, bending and screaming, they moved without a moment's cessation, while the beating of the tomtoms and the clanging of the cymbals grew quicker so imperceptibly that one was hardly aware of it.

The crowd, feeling the sweeping in of the emotion which was being roused in the most primitive way, swayed with the dancers, their eyes suffused with an insane light, their voices calling the wild, frenzy provoking "lu-lu-lu," that maddening challenge of the women that drove the dancers to greater efforts of physical demonstration.

By late afternoon the whole vast concourse was as one demented spirit split into a hundred thousand units of expression. Dusk found them staggering like abandoned creatures of an unbelievable world until the flare of torches lit up their bloodshot eyes, glistened off their sweating bodies. And still that terrible "lu-lu-lu" went throbbing upon the dusty air as the women reached the very crescendo of passionate dementia.

Then came the culmination in an orgy that beggars description.

Despite the apparently aimless moving of the vast crowd, there had been a steady guiding by the horsemen all through the hours of the day. And when the lights came smoking along in their hundreds and thousands, shutting out the purity of a wonderful moon, the dancers had been herded together in a wide square. There live sheep and goats were thrown in among the devotees. Upon the terrified animals they pounced with terrible cries, tearing at their throats with their teeth until great spurts of crimson burst over them.

The sight of the blood broke the last shred of control. A wild, indescribable cry rose from a hundred thousand throats, and then followed a scene that cannot be described.

Iron flails, axes, knives, knotted lengths of chain, and every conceivable tool of torture were flung about, while the pandemonium rose to an even higher pitch, until the whole scene was one of streaming blood and sweat under the flares—until a tall, bearded man who had been standing in a shadowy spot on the outskirts of the mob turned away, his eyes flickering in a disgust he could not keep down any longer.

This pilgrim had been in the city for some days. He had arrived in the fashion of a man of wealth, riding astride a sturdy hill pony, and attended by half a dozen servants. No Fezzi was more suave of manner than this man of the forked beard; no rich merchant from Tunis wore a more snowy burnous than he.

He was a man to attract attention even among those fanatical multitudes, and when he passed the savage men from the Jabala and the Rif, it was plain that he was a person of some consequence, for even those warriors salaamed in deep respect, murmuring, when he passed:

"It is Sakr-el-Droog, the Hawk of the Peak, he who was the right-hand man and captain of the front line fighting men of the Lion. We have fought under him. He is a devout follower of the one and only Prophet, and he has come here for the feast of Mulud."

It was indeed Sakr-el-Droog, the Hawk of the Peak, who had fallen from power when the Lion of the Rif—Abdel-Krim —

surrendered to the French; but he had not come to Meknes to celebrate the feast of Mulud despite the fact that, for private advancement, he had outwardly embraced Mahommedanism when he had jointed Abdel-Krim. What those fanatics would have said had they known that he was not the fair-skinned Moor he appeared to be, but a renegade Englishman whose name was George Marsden Plummer, it is difficult to say. At most he would have done well to escape from the stronghold of the Aissawa with a whole skin.

But Plummer was fully aware of the risk he ran in being in Meknes at such a time. He knew full well what would follow on his discovery—if he were discovered. Yet he had little fear of this. Although there were many men there from the Jabala and the Rif— even some who had fought under him— there had been very few persons in Abdel-Krim's entourage who had known that Sakr-el-Droog was other than what he seemed—a Moor of mighty prowess in battle.

Nor had Plummer come here through any devout wish to celebrate the natal day of the Prophet. He was there because the coast of Morocco was closed to him. He had been mixed up in an unfortunate business not long before in Tangier that had made the place too hot to hold him. He dared not go into Europe without sufficient means to see him through any complications that might arise, and, truth to tell, he had very little money.

It was through no love of Meknes that he was present on the scene. Rather was it a desperate gamble to try and turn something to his own advantage at a time when the place would be packed with pilgrims, and the chances of prey for the hawk would be many. Plummer was not the only person there with that aim in view.

He was not squeamish. He had witnessed sanguinary sights many a time, but there was something about the bestial abandon of this orgy here that sickened him. He knew that the place would be impossible for movement until after midnight, so once he was away from the mob, he turned his footsteps in the direction of the flat-roofed house which he had taken for the duration of his stay in Meknes. A man of his standing found it necessary to house himself in some style, for it is by outward appearances that a man is judged among those people.

This house was one of many which were occupied only during the feast of Mulud. It stood in a comparatively quiet quarter of the place close to the wonderful Aguedal gardens, which cover half the whole area of Meknes. The houses, like the gardens and the unfinished palace, with its half-hundred rooms—the adjacent stabling was intended to accommodate two thousand horses—were built by the most ambitious sultan Meknes ever knew, the notorious Mulay Ismail, who reigned more than two hundred years ago, and beside whom Abdel-Krim stands as but a ragged adventurer.

It was the ambition of Mulay Ismail to build a place that would rival the wonderful palace at Versailles, which Louis XIV conceived, and, indeed, one is told that the Moor even had the audacity to make an offer for the hand of the daughter of Le Roi Soleil. Be that as it may, the palace, with the magnificent gardens lying green and colourful against a blue sky that is a wonderful background to the fourteen minarets that rise above the city, are there to-day, together with nearly thirty miles of walls built by the Christian slaves whom Mulay Ismail had taken captive at one time or another.

And the smaller residences, built for Mulay Ismail's guests, have come in useful as places of abode for the rich merchants and sheiks who follow the less important devotees to the shrine of Sidi ben Aissa.

Once away from the great open space where the fanatics were still mutilating themselves in a frenzy that was wilder than that of any dervisn, the sound became muffled, and the smell of fetid bodies and noisome dust no longer filled the nostrils. It was only here and there that a light showed, but that was a relief to the tall, white-robed figure, for overhead sailed a glorious moon that made soft play of light over the gardens and white houses which lay still and ghostly and silent. It seemed incredible that so much beauty could be profaned by the atavistic orgy which was proceeding such a little distance away.

From near the gardens Plummer turned into a narrow, dusty street that led between a row of houses and high-trailed private gardens exactly similar to that which he was occupying. In fact, his own place was in this street —almost the last down on the left-hand side before the road branched into a less desirable thoroughfare leading to one of the bazaars.

Outwardly the places were as devoid of light as tombs, and as silent. But Plummer knew very well that there would be women of the harem on the flat roofs, concealed from the view of passers-by and those on other roofs, by grilles or lattices. The women from those houses would not, of course, take any part in the frenzied madness which had been let loose that day, but they would sit and listen, gossip and suck sweets, fan themselves and play with the jewels about their fat necks. Children in mind, all of them, and yet great lovers for intrigue.

The soft crunch of the tall Moor's sandals on the dust was enough to bring soft, fleshy forms stealing to the lattices at the front of the building, and for dark, curious eyes to watch this stern-looking chief who occupied one of the houses of the rich, and yet had brought no harem with him—a very strange thing indeed, and enough to give those in the harems of the other houses unlimited scope for gossip.

Nor could they satisfy their curiosity as to his identity, for to mention the matter to their own particular lords would have brought down fearful wrath upon them. They were not supposed to know of the existence of this man, for all men but one were taboo.

Plummer walked purposefully. The orgy of the chief festivities would be over this night, and on the morrow matters would settle down where business might be done. But what business was there for him? Nothing! Since he had been there he had used his ears and eyes to every possible effect, and yet he had failed to scent out a single thing that offered any promise.

There would be chance of small pickings, he knew. There always were, but he could not see himself joining the swarm of petty carrion in that scramble. There had been times in his life when he had stooped even lower than that; but several years with Abdel-Krim in the Rif had taught him what looting could be when the game was played for high stakes. Krim had fallen, but he had handled an enormous amount of wealth while he had wielded power.

And Plummer figured he was shrewd enough and knew his way about Morocco well enough to pick up a nice thing before he shook the dust of the place from his feet. He was pining for the flesh-pots of civilisation. He was dry for a drink of the life of Paris and London. He wanted to get once more into black evening clothes and hear the clink of silver and glass such as were never used here. He wanted to have a beautiful woman sitting opposite him, he wanted to hear good music instead of the crazy thrumming of tomtoms. He wanted all that and more. He was suffering from homesickness, and only a breath of what he had once known would ease it.

But how? To return without means for moving quickly from the place would be madness. He was "wanted" in every capital in Europe. He was renegade of his own country. The first moment Sakr-el-Droog became George Marsden Plummer a hundred human bloodhounds would be after him. Without money he would be but a dodging, blundering fox with no chance of a decent run. But with money he'd give them a run and then fool them!

But how? And again—how?

Money there was in Morocco—in Meknes if he could only figure out some scheme to get hold of it. "Money" meant actual coin or jewels—anything that could be turned into money. It was all the same to Plummer. He had thrashed out in his mind a score of schemes. As Sakr-el-Droog he had a certain cachet among the men from the Jabala and the Rif, and this cachet was good enough to give him considerable standing in Meknes.

Also when it was known that he was the notorious Sakr-el-Droog who had been the Lion's captain of troops his prestige would be even greater. To clinch that he carried certain introductions from his old accomplice in Tangier, Beni Said, who was as rich and cunning an old rascal as moved in all Morocco. But where did that get him? He had discarded every plan that came to mind. He wanted something that would mean quick action and big returns.

If he had a reliable accomplice he would have considered having a shot at some of the sacred relics in the mosque of Sidi ben Aissa, for although Plummer carried out his daily devotions, praying five times like every other one of the faithful, the whole business was only a means to an end with him, and he would have rifled the tomb of the Prophet himself as cheerfully as he would have cracked a bank safe in London.

He was in a mood where he would have tackled a caravan if there had been any hope. But only raiders of the hills could indulge in that. He was in a savage mood, and wanted to think. Somehow he must figure out a scheme before the morrow. He had the equivalent of about a hundred pounds left, but what was that when he wanted and needed thousands?

On reaching the high, vaulted door that shut off his own house and garden from the street he paused and rapped thrice. Almost at once there was the rattle of a chain and a half-naked Riff lad stood aside, salaaming while he entered.

The boy was no follower of Sidi ben Aissa, therefore he had not been tempted to go into the town to see the doings there. He was a follower of the Prophet all right, but not of the Aissawan sect, and now that Abdel-Krim was gone he was content to follow Sakr-el-Droog. He had been mighty useful to Plummer, and it was something in that country to know that he could trust one servant to the hilt. The boy, Abdul, would have died for the Hawk of the Peak. As for the rest of Plummer's attendants, they had been absent since morning, and it was problematical when he would see them again.

He walked up the path and through a Moorish arch into the garden. From this courtyard there were doors opening into the house, or rather doorways. There were barred, glassless windows on the ground floor and the one above, and, farther on, a sort of wing which was the harem. But now those quarters were empty, and the high cornice of the next roof made it impossible for the women there to see into the courtyard where Plummer sat down. He had chosen a low inlaid chair close to a small fountain.

The moon, almost full, was now directly overhead, lighting up the whole place with a soft beauty that was lost on George Marsden Plummer. Had those cold rays glinted on pieces of gold it would have been a different matter.

There was a low tabouret beside the table on which Abdul had placed a large stone flagon and some native cakes bought in the bazaar. As a good Muslim, Plummer was not supposed to touch alcohol, but like many others of that faith he chose to honour the precept in the breach rather than in the observance. Nevertheless, none but Abdul and himself knew that the stone flagon contained whisky—as precious as drops of molten gold in that place, and brought with the greatest care all the way from Tangier.

There was a wide-necked, red earthen water-bottle and a glass, and into this latter Plummer poured a generous measure of the amber liquid. He added a very little of the water, then he drank deep and thirstily. It was not the wine his throat was craving that night, but it was better than the sickening sherbets and cordials of the bazaar.

Then he lighted a cigarette and leant back, his gaze idly wandering about the patio and then sweeping without interest along the windowless wall which separated the next house from him. He was mildly curious as to the identity of the person who was occupying that place. It had been empty two days before, but he knew that someone had arrived the previous night.

That morning when he had been drinking coffee in the patio he had heard voices from the roof of the women's quarter, but the matter held his interest for only a few minutes. He was too intent on figuring out some scheme to extract a bunch of loot from Meknes to worry about neighbours.

His gaze came back to the fountain, then mechanically he reached out for his glass, was on the point of lifting it to his lips when his eye caught the flight of some small object just above him as it soared over the jet of water and landed with a soft "plop" at his feet.

Frowning in a puzzled way, wondering whence it had come, he bent down. His fingers closed on something soft, and then he held it up. His eyes narrowed still more as he saw it was a little bag of blue silk heavily embroidered with silver beads.

CHAPTER 2. A Queer Message from an Eastern Beauty— Plummer Answers in Person.

PLUMMER was deeply amazed and frankly intrigued.

As far as he knew, Abdul and he were the only persons in the place, and certainly the Rifi lad would never so far forget himself as to pitch anything at his master in this fashion. Besides, Abdul was at the back, in the kitchen quarters, getting a fire going against his master's need for food.

Then whence had come this embroidered trifle? And who had thrown it? Allowing that he was right about his own house, there was only one spot from which it could have travelled in order to come over the jet of water as it had and fall at his feet. That was the next house—that place from where he sat, was nothing but a blank, white wall.

He glanced in that direction, his eyes travelling on towards the harem quarter while his fingers fumbled with the trifle. There was something inside. He could feel something that seemed as if it might be folded paper. But he did not pull it out at once. Instead, he rose and, with the bag held in his hand so that the moonlight fell on it, walked round the fountain and stood in the middle of the court.

Once more his eyes wandered towards the high cornice and the lattice which he could just see above the roof of the harem belonging to the other house. But not a sign of any sort was there. If it had come from there, then the person who had thrown it had either done so through pure mischief, or for some reason which might or might not be a desire for intrigue with the tall, handsome Moor who travelled alone.

But George Marsden Plummer was not embarking upon any such perilous course as that. And it was because he thought this must be the case that his interest was not very active as he returned to his seat and opened the mouth of the little bag. It was such an affair as a woman might carry a powder-puff in, and two fingers were sufficient to catch hold of and draw out what it contained. When he saw that it was a folded piece of paper, he felt more certain than ever it was the signal for some silly intrigue.

Plummer needed no other light but the moon to read what was written on that folded piece of paper. As he straightened it out he saw at once that it was worded in French—a language he knew almost as well as his own. His interest was still sluggish as he began to read, but when he had comprehended the few words his eyes were a-glitter with sudden curiosity.

It might be only what he had at first thought it to be; but, on the other hand, there was, in the tone, something that told him it was no woman of the country who had written it. And if not—well, one never knew. That it was from a woman there could be no doubt. This was the brief message that had fallen at his feet:

"Monsieur,—I am quite sure that you are the great Sakr-el-Droog whom I once saw in Tangier—is it not? And, therefore, you will not find it difficult to recognise a certain name if I give you the initials G. M. P. I can see you when you sit by the fountain in your courtyard, but it is unwise that I show myself to you. Soon after midnight a silken ladder will be dropped from the roof of the house which faces you. Come up that ladder, monsieur— come, if you are brave, for adventure and perhaps other things that you seek."

• •   •   •

That was all; no signature—nothing to indicate whether it was only an invitation to harem intrigue or, as it hinted, to other things which might prove materially profitable. And that was the only sort of intrigue that held any interest just then for George Marsden Plummer.

"G. M. P," he muttered to himself "That means me all right. Now, who, among many women of this country, suspects that Sakr-el-Droog is not a Moor? I don't know of one. Certainly none of the baggages in the Rif ever suspected the truth. Then it must be someone from outside Morocco. The French wording tells little; it is the lingua franca of so much of the country. But if it isn't a Moorish woman, then what the dickens is a foreign woman doing here in Melenes at a time like this? If she has a male protector with her, who is he? This needs careful stepping, I can see that."

He measured that blank wall on the other side of the court with his gaze, but there was absolutely nothing to tell him whether someone was on the roof or not. He had a hunch, though, that he was very likely under a close scrutiny, so, somewhat ostentatiously, he took out a box of matches, selected one, and touched the flame to the bit of paper. When it had burned to a charred mass he dropped it on the tiles and ground his sandalled foot upon it.

Then he took the embroidered bag and placed it inside his voluminous white garments. If the woman who had written the note were watching, those actions should be sufficient to tell her that he was "on."

He drew out his watch, and saw that it was getting on for midnight. It occurred to him that his other servants might be returning at any time now, and, as he decided that it would be wiser if they knew nothing of his assignation, he walked to the front portal and slid all the bolts into place, hitching up the chain as an extra precaution. Abdul must have heard the sounds, for he came running along through the court just as Plummer was walking back.

"You will leave the bolts as they are," said Plummer curtly. "Those dogs of the desert can lie in the road until morning."

"It shall be, master," answered the boy who was only too pleased at the prospect of the others being forced to squat in the dust outside until it pleased his master to give the order for their admittance. Then; "Will the master take food now? His servant has prepared a fire, and the kous-kous is ready."

But Plummer shook his head.

"Not now. Keep the fires going. I am not hungry. I shall remain in my room on the upper floor for a little. Be within call, Abdul; I may want you."

Plummer passed through a pointed, arched opening into a bare, stone-flagged hall which was lit by a single oil dip. He continued his way to a smaller courtyard that lay between the main house and the kitchen quarters, and there mounted a flight of white-washed steps that ran against the outside wall to the floor above. There was a landing and opening, but, if he had desired, he could have continued on by a second flight to the flat roof.

There were no lights any sort on this floor, but, with the exception of the passage that ran from back to front, the rooms were illuminated enough for one to move about by the moon, Plummer pushed aside some hanging curtains, and entered the room he had been occupying as a bedroom. Everything in the place was white from the wash that had been spread with a lavish hand, and that helped him to see.

There was no glass in the window, but the opening had half a dozen strong wooden bars set in the framework. It was this window that was Plummer's objective, for, although it was on a slightly lower level than the roof of the next house, it gave him a fairly good view of the lattice-work which ran round above the cornice.

But he did not show himself at the window. Instead, he kept close to one wall, working his way round until he was in the corner to the left of the window. There he sank down until he was on hands and knees, and in this fashion crept across until he could squat in a patch of shadow, out of sight of anyone who might chance to peer across, and yet could see almost the full stretch of the lattice-work opposite.

And there he remained, motionless as any Moor who had generations of patience born in him as a very part of his nature. He wanted to see if the person who had written the note would reveal any impatience—any curiosity to see what was going on.

From time to time he glanced at his watch. Midnight came, and still no sign from the other house. Ten minutes passed, and the night was a White silence. Even Abdul had sunk down somewhere at the back to drowse while waiting on his master's pleasure. Not even a distant murmur now came from the packed multitudes he had left in the square.

A quarter-past twelve. He began to ask himself if the whole thing was only a hoax after all, when suddenly there came a slight clicking sound, and as he leant forward ever so little, he saw a small portion of the lattice-work swing inwards. Then a bare, white arm emerged—the rounded, supple arm of a woman, and one that could only be young to possess such firmness of flesh. It waved to and fro for a moment or two, then something swished snakily down against the white wall and struck with a subdued "plop" on the tiles.

Plummer could just make out the regular cross and upright pattern against the whitewashed wall; it was the silken ladder. Then the opening in the lattice closed without a sound.

He rose cautiously, and slipped his burnous from him. Standing now, he was clad in a white, shirt-like tunic, richly edged with gold braid. He wore white trousers, which were held up by a carelessly tied sash of the same colour. He was wearing no turban on his head, but a round velvet cap of blue, embroidered with silver.

Tall as he was, with dark skin and pointed beard, he was certainly a picturesque-looking figure—an arresting personality at any time. Nor was his savage dash lessened by the hilt of the long-bladed knife that was thrust carelessly into his sash, its red leather hilt contrasted in silent menace against the white of his sash.

He had rid himself of his burnous for two reasons. One was that he should climb the easier; the other was to be free for movement in case a trap was waiting for him on the opposite roof. And there was just one other precaution he took. Crossing to the sleeping-mat where his blankets and meagre personal belongings lay rolled up, he took out a small holster and loosened an automatic pistol. Scrutinising this to see that the clip was in order, and a cartridge in the breech, he placed it inside his shirt where he could reach it quickly. Then he was ready.

When he had descended to the lower floor he gave a low whistle that brought Abdul on the run. Plummer caught him by the shoulder.

"Pay heed," he whispered. "I go to the house which touches our court. Be on the watch. I may return quickly or I may remain some time. But in no case are the other servants to be admitted if they hammer on the outer door. You understand?"

"It is an order to thy slave, master."

Plummer dropped his hand and walked through the gloomy hall, followed discreetly by Abdul, whose dark eyes were full of excitement. This was the sort of thing that he loved. It meant, he hoped, that profit and other things were to come their way. The native boy knew his master in a shrewd way, and he was the sort of master who gave generously when money was plentiful.

Plummer strode out into the courtyard in an unhurried way. Passing the fountain he allowed his eyes to lift once to the roof of the house he was approaching. But beyond that thin, silken ladder hanging against the white wall there was nothing to indicate that anything had happened since he had been sitting by the fountain.

Then he was at the bottom of the ladder, his hands gripping the side strands. He hesitated only a moment, looking back to catch sight of Abdul lurking in the shadows, then knowing the lad would be on watch every moment, he started to climb.

It is not easy, working one's way upwards on a loose, hanging cord ladder. One's toes continually come into contact with the wall and, unlike a ladder made of firm uprights such as wood or bamboo, there is no bottom purchase. But George Marsden Plummer had swarmed up too many ropes in his time and had pulled off too many second-story jobs to be worried by a perfectly good silken ladder.

He went up steadily, picking his foothold easily with his toes, until his hands were on a level with the coping of the roof. Then his fingers were catching holes of the openings in the lattice, and just as his head came above the coping the wicket in the lattice swung open.

14

He caught a fleeting glimpse of the same rounded white arm, then it was lost in the shadow, and he heard a whisper saying:

"Come through, please; there is nothing in your way."

Plummer managed with some little difficulty to squeeze through the opening. He still kept hold of the lattice until his feet found a soft purchase; then he released his grasp and stood upright.

At first he could see no one. On this side of the court the moonlight was only a reflected paleness from the white outside.

He seemed to be standing in a sort of narrow passage, and he knew that the person who owned that round, white arm could not be far away. He took a tentative step forward, and in the same instant the wicket closed behind him.

A faint, very subtle odour drifted into his nostrils. Plummer was an expert in scents, and he knew this elusive waft at once as that very rare and extremely expensive essence known as "moi-meme." In all the world there was just one shop in Paris where it could be got. That was something to go on with and, to him, a decided relief from the musk which he had half expected.

Suddenly something touched his arm, urging him forward. He pushed in against soft curtains, passed, between them, found himself in complete darkness, then more curtains, and after that a large, low-ceilinged apartment, such as never in his life had he seen before.

It was lighted by three jade water lamps, beneath which he saw a confusion of colour on every side. Low, wide divans which were a mass of greens and blacks and golds; rich rugs and wall hangings that would have fetched a fabulous price in the marts of the west; low stands and tabourets, on which were scattered in careless profusion gold-jointed dragons and jade slabs, alabaster and coral; feathered plumage of egrets and kingfisher and bird of paradise; some wonderful things from as far east as the Sudan; a perfect riot of red and black pots of paint and essences—a wonderful bizarre place that seemed to have nothing but throbbing colour.

Plummer turned slowly to see just what sort of person could fit into such a setting. He had heard a soft rustle behind him, and now something moved just under the central jade water lamp. He took a step forward, and then paused, literally gasping, as his eyes fell on the woman who posed in that flood of green.

She was dressed in jacket and harem pantaloons of heavy silk. The colour might have been jade, like the bowls of the water lamps, or peacock blue. One couldn't tell in that green flood. But her hair was black as a moonless night; her eyes direct, dark, fathomless pools, provoking, compelling, beautiful, mocking, and as soulless as two marbles.

They seemed to be so slightly oblique giving an Oriental touch to the face, but that impression may have been accentuated by the very smooth whiteness of the brow.

Her nose was short and straight, her mouth as red as a clove rose. Her throat was white and beautifully pillared on her shoulders, bare but for a great emerald that hung from a thin, gold chain.

George Marsden Plummer had seen many women in his time, but never had his eyes rested on anything like this. He thought he could place every one he had ever seen in her proper niche; but he had never been up against such a complete enigma as the silken-clad creature who posed before him—the faintest hint of mockery in her sloe-coloured eyes. He felt as if he had been whisked away into some place of dreams, and he knew he must orientate himself. He relaxed, so to speak, and took a step towards her.

"Who are you?" he asked in a low tone. "What do you want with me?"

CHAPTER 3.   Plummer is Baffled— The Pine Sacred Tokens.

SHE smiled at him—a slow, unfathomable, baffling smile.

"So you came, Mr. Plummer," she said in low tones of rich liquid timbre. Nor was Plummer less puzzled by her using English and his name. "Come and sit down," she went on, turning away. "I want to talk to you." Plummer followed her across the extraordinary apartment towards one of the divans. Despite the fact that the tunic of her silk harem dress was cut in straight lines he could see the supple curves of her body as she walked.

She sank on to one of the divans and motioned for Plummer to come beside her. Then she pushed forward a little tabouret on which had been placed cigarettes — thin sobrames, Plummer discovered. When he had held a silver lighter for her and had touched the flame to his own, she shot a side-long glance at him. Then she laughed softly.

"And you have come," she repeated. "I watched you read my little note, monsieur."

Plummer was quite prepared to dally with this exquisite creature once he knew on what ground he stood; but until then he was going to be very wary. There was no telling what this house might contain. At the thought his hand unconsciously slid to the hilt of his knife. The woman saw the movement and laughed again.

"There is nothing to fear, Mr. Plummer," she said. "This place is not a trap."

"One moment, madame," he answered. "When you speak I shall be obliged if you will address me as Sakr-el-Droog, while I am in Meknes. And now, perhaps, you will be good enough to tell me why you asked me to come here. I can understand that it is my privilege to be admitted to your presence, but —" and he shrugged.

"But you think I have a stronger reason than a mere flirtation with you. You are correct, Sakr-el-Droog. And that should be so, for you see I have followed you all the way from Paris."

He looked genuinely surprised.

"From Paris? But why was that necessary?"

"Because I wished to see you— urgently. I came to Tangier. I had a letter to one Beni-Said there. Now you can guess how I knew that you had come to Meknes."

"That is reasonable. Beni-Said knew my whereabouts."

"And he told me. I heard, too, that your plans had been a little

17

upset lately. I was sorry for your sake, but glad for mine, for I said to myself he may be more willing now to listen to me. You see, monsieur, I have heard quite a lot about you; and that is why I have been seeking you. It needs a steady nerve, a resourceful mind and a cool head to do what I wish done."

"You are most flattering, madame, but please remember that I am most unfortunate in not knowing with whom I am speaking."

"You have been away from Europe for some years, monsieur."

"I have been in the Rif during the past eight years, but I have been in Paris and London during that time. I did not advertise my movements, madame."

"But you did not remain long. Perhaps you have been a little out of touch with things. But, perhaps, you have been kept informed. If you have, then it may be you have heard of her who has been called the Bird of Paradise. It is a name not unknown in Paris."

Plummer looked at her with renewed interest.

"The Bird of Paradise—I have heard that name used in reference to an actress who carried Paris by storm two or three years ago. Are you she, madame?"

"I have been so called, monsieur." Plummer could believe it. Every bit of her was as exotic as the brilliant and colourful bird which hangs in the sun among the Spice Islands of the East. As he saw her now, it was, indeed, a fitting name. But if she spoke the truth if she was, indeed, the actress known by that name, who had sent all Paris raving a short time before, then what was she doing in a place like Meknes? And what did she want of him?

It must be something of a very important nature to her mind, to send her on a long trek like this. And if she needed someone of his sort, why had she not chosen from among the scores of people in Paris, who would be only too willing to serve her?

She was watching him and in an uncanny way seemed to know exactly what was going on in his mind so well, indeed, that her words startled him.

"I will answer your thought, monsieur. I sought you, instead of choosing among others, because I knew that Sakr-el-Droog was the man for my work. I have something of your past, monsieur; I know that when you set out to accomplish a thing you allow nothing to stand in your way. That is the sort of man I need."

"It must be something you desire very dearly," remarked

Plummer slowly. "I have always understood that the Bird of Paradise could command great wealth if she but snapped her fingers."

She made a moue of distaste.

"Poof! That is true. But if one takes wealth, monsieur, one must needs take what goes with it. And the Bird of Paradise is not to be bought. What she yields can only be given freely. I have this great wish—I need a man such as Sakr-el-Droog; I throw up everything in Paris and go to seek him."

"You mean you have cast aside your contracts there?"

"Of course. What I desire is much more than that. I need you, monsieur —will you join me? The reward will be as great—in every way—as you could wish."

Plummer's eyes rested on hers. He couldn't read anything definite in them. They were completely baffling, and yet they seemed to tell him that now, in all his life, was the supreme moment for him to make a decision on which his whole future would rest. Out of the fanatical din of Meknes this had come to him.

"What is it you wish of me?" he asked at last.

She leant forward a little so that the faint breath of her swept over him. He was getting "heady," but he was keeping his wits about him.

"Monsieur," she said, in a low tone, " have you ever heard of the Five Pearl Thimbles of Chen-tse?"

George Marsden Plummer jerked the upper part of his body round as if someone had jabbed him with the point of a knife. His eyes narrowed, and he leant forward, his breath coming more quickly.

"The Five Pearl Thimbles of Chen-tse," he whispered. "What—do—you—know—about—them?"

"Your attention is arrested, monsieur, I know now that you have heard of them. Have you ever seen them, Sakr-el-Droog?"

"Yes; once!"

He seemed to be speaking now like an automaton.

"In—China?"

"Yes; in China,"

"Where, monsieur?"

"In the Temple of Eternal Purity, by the Gate of the Tiger, in Canton."

"Ah!"

As the low exclamation broke from her she put out one hand and laid it on his arm. Her lids had dropped, and her nostrils were quivering.

"Then I have not been misinformed; you have seen them."

"Who has told you this? It is for that reason you have sought me out?"

"Yes. Listen, monsieur. Some months ago, in Paris, I was pestered much by a man from the East. He was a Celestial—a Chinois—of princely rank. He gave me no peace; it was impossible for me to go abroad that he did not follow me. He sent me jewels — such jewels! He offered me everything of his wealth, and I laughed at him. But at last I consented to receive him. I would have none of his gifts, for he was a Manchu, and—I hate the Manchus. I will conceal nothing from you, monsieur. You may have heard great mystery about the Bird of Paradise. She has been said to belong to many different races. But they have always been wrong. Some day I may tell you the whole truth of that, but not now. It is enough to say that I have been in China. I, too, have seen the Five Pearl Thimbles of Chen-tse. Oh!"

She closed her eyes and swayed towards him. Plummer had sworn not to let himself yield to the dangerous influence of her; but his arm went out, and she sank against it. He turned his head away. He kept telling himself that he must keep his balance; he must allow nothing of the maddening appeal of her to influence him; and yet mortal man could not hold that supple, warm body so close and keep his senses clear. He was both glad and sorry when she murmured something and drew away from him.

He was thinking fast. She had just said that she, too, had seen the Five Pearl Thimbles of Chen-tse. How could that be? No women were ever allowed in the Temple of Eternal Purity. Moreover, the Five Pearl Thimbles of Chen-tse were of such a sacred nature that only the keeper of the temple treasures had access to them. Probably not a score of living Chinese had ever set eyes on the sacred tokens. Then how could it be that this woman beside him had seen them? And how did she know that he had ever set eyes on them?

How Plummer had actually glimpsed those wonderful gems, is a story of his early career of crime. He had struck high when he had tried to filch those fabulous gems from the Temple of Eternal Purity. He had seen them; that is all. It was lucky for him that he had got away when he did. By the space of a few seconds he had eluded capture, and, had that been his portion, he would have gone to such torture as only the Chinese have been able to evolve over untold centuries.

He shivered now when he thought of it. It was uncanny, this reminder of the past. He felt a twinge of nervous doubt as he looked at her again. Plummer was no coward, but that incident was one which he had thought long buried.

"You have said something, madame, that must be explained," he said slowly. "How did you know that I had ever seen the Five Pearl Thimbles?"

"Because I was there at the time," she whispered, as if every word was dragged from her.

"You were there? But that is impossible! No women— You could have been but a little girl! You are joking, madame. None of your sex have access to that part of the temple."

She faced him, her eyes so shadowy that they seemed to fill the hollows.

"You forget, monsieur, that there is one class of my sex in the keeper's portion of the temple."

A soft imprecation escaped him.

"You mean—you mean the temple girls?" he stammered.

She bent her head.

"And you—you were one of those girls?"

"From infancy, monsieur."

"But I do not understand. You are not Chinese? Only the children of the 'High-Born' are admitted to the temple as attendants upon the Buddha."

"Chinese girls of the 'High-Born,' or girls of your race, monsieur, if they can be secured. I had not intended telling you more of this; but now I must. I cannot disclose all. I am of your race, and of the other, too. I was stolen as an infant from the foreign settlement in Shanghai. How I was taken down the coast to Canton I do not know. Nor do I remember anything of my life before I was of the temple. I have learned since then —in many ways which it would take too long to explain here. There are many secret passages in the temple. The girls who attend upon the Buddha know some of them. The keeper is old; it is said he has been there for much more than a hundred years. We wandered about with a certain degree of freedom, and I was in a secret niche behind the inner altar of the Buddha on the night you came. I knew little then. There were many whispers, and your name was spoken many times." Plummer knew that his identity had been discovered, and her words sounded like the truth. "The affair made a deep impression upon me. I watched you when you found the hidden place where the Five Pearl Thimbles lay. I heard your gasp of wonder as you looked upon them; and I heard, too, the sound that caused you to flee without them. You were wise, monsieur; you would have known a terrible fate had you remained."

"By Heaven! I believe you did see!" broke in the man excitedly, for her words had brought back vividly the picture of what had happened that night in Canton. It seemed he must be dreaming; it was incredible that he could be sitting here in a room in the heart of Morocco listening to that tale from a woman who had been a temple girl in Canton. He passed a hand across his brow. "What—what else?" he stammered.

"I have spoken of the Chinois who pestered me in Paris. He did not know that I had ever been of the Temple of Eternal Purity. No one knows that. How I escaped does not matter. I succeeded, and I took with me sufficient gold to bring me to Europe. Have you ever seen me dance, monsieur?"

"No; I regret it."

"Had you done so, you would, perhaps, have seen things that reminded you of China. If anyone knew the truth my life would not be worth that!" And she snapped her fingers. "But they think I was drowned in the river. I had put it all away from me. I was forgetting, when the Chinois came to remind me. And then, monsieur, when he babbled of his love, he talked of many things. He spoke of—"

"The Five Pearl Thimbles of Chen-tse."

"Yes. He was breaking the most sacred oath, monsieur. I listened, and led him on. He was, he said, a near relative of the Keeper of the Treasure. He promised me, if I would yield to him, that he would give me those five pearls."

"He was mad. How could he do that?"

"I asked him. He said he would return to China and get them. I did not believe him. There was something deeper behind it all. I was curious —more than inquisitive, monsieur. I began to suspect—I began to realise what horror lay ahead for him and for anyone who might become identified with him. I grew afraid, monsieur."

"I understand. He must have been mad!"

She did not answer at once. For some moments she sat

motionless, her eyes resting on his, then she nodded thrice.

"He was mad, monsieur, because he did not need to return to China to get the Five Pearl Thimbles of Chen-tse."

Plummer ground the end of his cigarette in a tray. He was using every atom of will power to appear nonchalant. But his blood was racing wildly. If she meant what he thought she meant—

"I mean, monsieur, that they are in Europe!"

CHAPTER 4. Plummer and Vali Mata-Vali Join Forces— The Combined Caravan—Mutiny and Attach in the Desert.

THE sensuous nearness of her meant nothing to Plummer now. Even predatory instinct was roused— everything in him that had made him what he was. Years before, when he had been one of the crack men at Scotland Yard, it had been the same "hunting" streak in his nature that had lifted him into the front rank. It had been sheer chance that he had discovered the truth about himself— had suddenly realised it wasn't men he wanted to hunt down, but loot.

His position at the time had given him many advantages to prosecute this desire, and for a long time he successfully raced with the hares and followed with the hounds. But the inevitable had occurred. The sensation which swept over police circles when George Marsden Plummer was unmasked is not yet forgotten. And from that moment, when he was forced definitely to ally himself openly with the criminal ranks, he had prosecuted his crooked ways with gusto.

No more ruthless criminal was abroad than Plummer; no crook had ever aimed higher than he. Prison walls had held him again and again, and, some years before, when he had entirely disappeared, it was believed that he was dead. All the evidence seemed indisputable. But he had been unmasked once more by Sexton Blake as Sakr-el-Droog, the right-hand man of Abdel-Krim, the Lion of the Rif. He had made half a dozen fortunes while with Abdel-Krim, and he had spent them.

Plummer never would hold money; he loved the fleshpots too well. And now this startling information had come to him at a time when he was casting about desperately for some way in which to make a big turn. Abdel-Krim was gone. For Plummer, Morocco was worked out.

His going to Meknes had been a last, desperate cast of the dice, in order to try to win a stake to take him out of Morocco. Little had he dreamed that there, in that haunt of Aissawaa fanatics, he was to hear news of the Five Pearl Thimbles of Chen-tse.

It was true that not more than three or four Europeans knew even of the existence of those unbelievably wonderful pearls; and it was equally true that not more than a score of initiated Chinese had ever seen them. They were the highest symbol in all Buddhism in China. No one knew how long they had been guarded in the inner shrine of the Temple of Eternal Purity by the Gate of the Tiger In Canton.

The ancient records of the temple might have shown, and, indeed, they did show, that they had been there long before the Buddhist faith had had its birth. They had belonged to some earlier religious ritual, thousands of years before the hordes of Europe had emerged from the skin and woad stage.

And Plummer had seen them. Never in all his career of crime had he been so near touching the ultimate prize. But at the very moment of triumph they had eluded him. If one could but get them—there was no greater prize in all the world—they were worth anything, anything at all.

With just one of those giant pearls one could buy luxury for life; with two, a perfect pair, one could step into the ranks of the very rich. And then one could have three in reserve. It seemed to Plummer that the woman could not be correctly informed. The Five Pearl Thimbles of Chen-tse in Europe!

It could not be. Who could have succeeded in abstracting them from the inner shrine of the temple, where they had lain so well secreted. It was not possible. The woman—this aptly called Bird of Paradise—might be sincere enough in her statement. She would not have cut all her contracts in Paris and set out to find him just to excite him by some will-o'-the-wisp. And yet—

"I don't understand," he said at last heavily. "It is not possible, surely, madame."

"I don't blame you for doubting, monsieur. I should do the same. But listen. I know they are in Europe. This Chinois, of whom I spoke—one night he was deep in opium and he— talked. I drew him out. He promised everything if I would return to China with him as first wife of his household. And then he began to tell me of the most wonderful pearls in the world which he would give me. He spoke of the number—five—and, from other words he used, I began to wonder. I needed to use care, monsieur, but I know how to make men talk. And from step to step, I guided his tongue until I knew! No other woman would have realised what he meant. But I had been of the temple; I had seen the Five Pearl Thimbles of Chen-tse, and I knew! I was breathless with fear, even to have him near me, monsieur.

"From the moment those sacred symbols were taken every resource of the priests of that temple would be set in motion to find the man who had committed this terrible desecration. No word would leak out. But they must be recovered at any cost. And this man—this Manchu of the 'High-Born' had done that thing. Even in the foolishness of the opium he spoke guardedly. It was as if some inner spirit were warning him, and any other woman would have thought only that he spoke of five particularly fine pearls.

"But it meant a different thing to me. I knew that this man had brought the Five Pearl Thimbles of Chen-tse to Paris. My heart almost stopped. I knew not what to do. There was terrible danger even to be near them. What should I do? I resolved to get them into my possession if I could. Then I would decide.

"If I could return them to the Temple of Eternal Purity, it would mean that no longer need I walk in fear of being discovered and taken back there; if I braved that horror and terror and kept them by me, what could I do with them? I made him believe that I would yield— when he gave me these wonderful pearls. He— he went to get them; he never returned. I do not know, monsieur, if you read of the terrible thing that was found running about among the wooded glades of the Bois in Paris some months ago. It was an awful discovery. I cannot speak of the horror of it. But that thing was the man who had stolen the Five Pearl Thimbles of Chen-tse."

She paused, and Plummer, who had been sitting as rigid as a poker, let a sibilant breath escape him. He had no doubts now; he believed. He knew what unnameable horrors must have been visited upon that wretch before he was turned loose as a mewling thing whose very soul had been destroyed.

"If he was found—if he was the thing that was found wandering in the Bois—I did read something of that— then the priests must have regained the pearls," he ventured thoughtfully.

"No. He was not alone in that conspiracy. I went to his house when he did not return. I found some things that gave me hints. I used every effort to unravel them. I succeeded to a certain extent. There were Europeans in that conspiracy with him. There were four of them; he made the fifth. He had lied to me when he had said he could give me the five pearls. He only had one and that was recovered by the priests. The other four are in the possession of his four companions. I have with me the papers I speak of. It will be difficult, but I believe it to be possible to find those four men, monsieur. The priests will still be looking for them, and when they find them—"

She broke off and shivered.

26

"Why have you come to me? Keep nothing back."

"I did not know what to do. And then I remembered you. I realised that you had been brave enough to enter the very heart of the temple in order to secure those pearls. I thought if I could find you! I could not get them out of my mind. Monsieur, if we could overtake those four men and secure the pearls it might be possible for us to remain unknown to the priests. Never was such glory in gems. You have seen and you know."

Plummer nodded. He was game enough to have a shot at running down the remaining four gems if he could get a lead that promised anything. She spoke of possessing certain clues. But it would need money—plenty of it to carry out such a hunt. And he had none or next to none.

"It is a temptation," he said at last. "I think I should be quite prepared to risk the priests, and if I could track down the four men who now have possession of the pearls I should get them all right—no matter what extreme steps had to be taken."

Her eyes glinted at his words, for she knew what he meant. But she held her peace, waiting for him to continue.

"I shall have to be frank," he went on. "While I was with Abdel-Krim there was plenty of money and loot. I spent a dozen fortunes, and a short time ago I thought I was going to get away with another. But it fell through, and, at the moment, madame, I have not the capital to follow up your proposal."

"But I have plenty of money, monsieur. I should not come to you and make this proposal without intending to do my share. I can finance everything. You may have whatever you ask for. I have come a long way to find you, monsieur; I have given careful thought to this. I am ready to embark upon anything with the right partner. And you," she added in a soft, caressing voice, "are the partner I have been seeking, Sakr-el-Droog. I want this to be more than ever since talking with you. We may fail, monsieur, but if we do there will be other things to go after. I am ready to give up my career. I am not old, and I am not ugly, monsieur, I think—I think you would not find your life unpleasant, monsieur."

Even now Plummer held himself in check. Years before he had sworn to himself that he would travel alone— that he would hunt as a lone wolf. Time and again he had seen men fall into the meshes of the police net through trusting women. Seldom had it been different. He was recalling now that in one case only had it not been that way. He was thinking of Huxton Rymer and Mary Trent.

But this exotic creature was different from any other woman he had ever known. She was intoxicating enough in her physical appeal; but more than that she had brains and nerve. She would, he knew, endorse any action it might be necessary to take. She would be as ruthless as he; she would have no regrets. If it was necessary to kill she would hand him the weapon or use it herself. Why not? he asked himself.

She knew well enough what was going on in his mind. She could see that he was wavering. Be sure she had not embarked upon this affair without learning a good deal about Plummer before she started. She knew that he had always hunted as a lone wolf; and that was one of the things that had influenced her. If she could make him yield, then there would be no other women to complicate matters. And the more she regarded them the more did she want him to say "yes."

She had come to Meknes prepared to make many concessions to persuade him to enter her service. She was beyond that now. She wanted him not to serve her, but to work with her— she was feeling now that she would serve him. He was the man she had been ready to yield to for years without realising it. Other men had thrown themselves at her feet, and had become maudlin. This man felt the sensuous appeal of her; she could see that. But still he kept himself in check, and his brain worked clearly.

She swayed forward, and one round, white arm went about his shoulder. Slowly, gently she drew him closer to her warm, supple body. Plummer bent his head and looked down at her. She raised her face so that her red lips were close to his, parted slightly in maddening invitation. His arm went suddenly about her; a thrill shot through him as the warmth of her penetrated to him. Then he swept her in close, and his head went down until his lips found hers.

Later, they discussed ways and means. Vali Mata-Vali was her name, she told him. The way she said it made the liquid syllables roll attractively to the ear. She was all eager to go as soon as possible. She had brought plenty of money with her. She opened a chest and showed Plummer heaps upon heaps of gold coins and packets of good English notes. He drew a deep breath as he gazed upon it. It was the sort or sight that he could appreciate.

She had brought her own caravan with twenty mounted men as a guard. It was a wonder she had got through safely. It would not do to go back by way of Tangier. The French and Spanish authorities there were too anxious to lay their hands on Sakr-el-Droog. But they could make directly west for the coast near Rabat. The town would have to be avoided for the same reason, but there was Sahli a little to the north. They could get some sort of craft at Sahli and make a French Biscayan port.

After that, Paris, where, it seemed, Vali had a large house at St. Cloud that would serve excellently as headquarters. It all looked to George Marsden Plummer as one of the most attractive propositions he had ever run up against; nor was Vali Mata-Vali the least part of that attraction.

It was nearly dawn when Plummer left her and swung himself down the silken ladder into his own courtyard. The moon was low in the sky now, but he could still hear the distant throb of a tomtom. He waved his hand to her, then, when she had drawn up the strand of silk and closed the lattice, he walked towards the fountain.

It seemed that the whole thing must have been some vision of the Arabian Nights. Here he was in Meknes in the heart of Morocco, and yet he might just have come from a room in China; here was the world of Allah, and the breath of Mahommed; up there had been the spirit of Buddha, and the vision of the Temple of Eternal Purity; the sloe-eyed beauty Vali Mata-Vali and talk of the Five Pearl Thimbles of Chen-tse.

Plummer got to work that same day. He did not lie down, but after a cold bath and rub down he once more assumed his burnous. Abdul, not a little curious, but thinking his master's visit to the adjoining house was nothing more than a harem escapade, served him with steaming coffee. When Plummer had drunk that and smoked a couple of cigarettes, he went along to the heavy door leading to the street, and unbolted it.

Outside in the road, lying in divers positions in an exhausted sleep were his house servants. He surveyed them with a sneer, then one by one he kicked them into a wakefulness. As he drove them into the courtyard, Abdul helped them along with the end of a leathern whip, and when that duty was finished, Plummer took himself off to the business part of the town.

His first duty was to find the active men of his caravan. It took considerable persuasion on his part, and the promise of double pay, to get them to agree to start off that same day. They had been counting on at least another three days of debauch in Meknes, but the colour of Sakr-el-Droog's gold clinched the argument. Then came the purchase of supplies. It was not a great distance to Sahli—something in the neighbourhood of a hundred miles, but part of the way was through a very dangerous district where the savage Berbers were accustomed to lie in wait for small caravans going to or coming from Fez and Meknes.

If the slightest whisper got out that there was a chest of gold passing through, every carrion in the mountains would be at the feast. Plummer was leaving it to Vali Mata-Vali to make her arrangements with her own caravan guards.

The two parties would travel as one, but not until they were outside the walls of Meknes would Sakr-el-Droog take command of the two parties. In this way he hoped to whittle down the inevitable friction and jealousy between the two companies.

He was back at his house a little after midday, and when he had received a signal from the next house, went out into the road and approached it quite openly. The Bird of Paradise had not been idle. She announced herself as ready to leave at whatever hour he named, so a rendezvous was fixed for half-past four on the outskirts of the market on the Fez road. This was the usual spot on which caravans started for Fez and Rabat.

By five o'clock they were moving off, Vali being veiled like any other Mahommedan woman, and riding pillion behind Plummer, who was mounted on a big, powerful Berber stallion, which he had ridden in from the Jabala country.

They did not propose to make a great distance that night. This was only a brief period before sunset, and even though they would have the benefit of the moon, Plummer was not anxious to pass through the danger zone except by daylight. So about seven o'clock they made camp in a small wadi about nine miles out of Meknes, and it was here that Plummer took full command of the outfit.

Had he been some ordinary merchant there would have been mutterings, and possibly worse. But the whole caravan knew him now as the dread Sakr-el-Droog, who had fought with such valour in the Rif, and that settled it.

He had a small, brown hide tent pitched for Vali. But he himself was content to roll his burnous about him and sleep on the sand as did the others. After the evening meal of dates and kous-kous, he and the woman talked in the shadow for a little, but she soon withdrew, and Plummer sought a place near the chest containing the money. That night passed without incident.

They were off again shortly after dawn, and kept up the trek until midday. They halted then for food, and to let the worst of the heat pass, but they moved off again at two, and by late afternoon they passed down the western slopes of the Atlas Mountains towards the coast. By the next afternoon they should glimpse the sea, and by the night after that should reach Sahli. That night when Vali had retired to her tent, Abdul came to Plummer.

"What is it?" asked Plummer, seeing by the boy's manner that he had something to communicate to him.

"There is talk among the men, master," he whispered. "Our men are all right, but the men of the lady make sly talk of money. I do not know what they mean, but it does not sound good."

That was enough to tell Plummer that his most immediate danger was from his own men; or, rather, from the men of Vali's caravan. In some way they guessed that there was actual coin specie in the caravan. They may have suspected this before reaching Meknes, and may have plotted to get it there or after Vali started to return.

Plummer's advent with his men would have upset their plans, but they must still be trying to figure out a way if they were talking as Abdul said. And George Marsden Plummer had not the slightest intention that they should get a single piece of that gold, other than the double pay which had been promised to them.

"Is that all, Abdul?"

"There is also talk, master, that some Berber horsemen were seen this afternoon,"

"Why was this not reported to me?" demanded Plummer sternly.

"Master, I did not see, and I have only just heard. It may not be true."

"You think they may betray us tonight?"

"Master, I think they mean mischief."

"Very well, Abdul. Return to your place. If you hear anything more or see signs of mutiny, give me the signal. I shall be ready."

"I'll go, master. If the master wills I shall take a rifle and use it if necessary."

"Go to my leader of the caravan. He will give you one. And make your way quietly among our own men. Tell them to see to their weapons. I can trust them; they know that Sakr-el-Droog is not to be trifled with."

"Master, it is done."

With that, Abdul stole off, and for some time Plummer lay back in the shadow as if dozing. But his wits were working fast, and at the end of half an hour or so he rose. He walked about this way and that, as if just making a formal inspection of the camp, but all the time he was working towards Vali's tent. Reaching the flap, he paused.

"Are you asleep?" he whispered in English.

"No. Is anything wrong?"

"I think mischief is brewing— among your men. There is nothing to be alarmed about, but it might be awkward if they try any tricks tonight. We are in the middle of the danger zone, and Abdul thinks we have been under the eyes of Berber spies this afternoon. I want you to keep to your tent no matter what happens."

"I shall, of course, obey you; but I'd much rather be at your side. I am not afraid."

"I am sure of that. But your place is here. I am going to slip out of the camp. I have a plan. I shall let it be known that I am going to scout over the edge of the wadi. But I shall make a quick detour and come in at the other side. If they are going to start something it will be when they think I am well away from the camp. But I shall be back before they can get well started. I know that my own Rifi men are all right. But no matter what happens don't look out, and don't allow anyone to enter your tent."

"I shall kill the first person who pushes that flap aside unless he speaks with your voice."

"Good girl! I am off now."

There was something in her voice that tempted him to enter and take her in his arms, if only for a moment. But he knew this was no time to yield to that sort of thing. A few minutes might make all the difference between success or failure of the mutiny.

He strode boldly through the camp, giving a meaning glance to the leader of his own men as he passed. He paused and said loudly:

"I am going scouting over the edge of the wadi. See that a good guard is kept while I am gone."

"It is done, master."

He saw that Vali's men were seated by themselves, and his quick eye noted, too, that each man was nursing his long-barreled rifle. It certainly looked as if Abdul was right. He saw the lad seated in the shadow, also fondling a rifle, and Plummer noted with inward satisfaction that the boy had it trained, apparently unconsciously, on the captain of Vali's men. He had a hunch Abdul would "get" that fellow quickly if he could.

Once he was outside the circle of the camp, Plummer moved across to where the camels squatted and the horses were tethered. He spoke a few words to the men on guard there, and then made straight for the rocky side of the ravine. The moon was now up, and he was plainly visible in his white garments as he climbed. Reaching the top, he went over quickly. To stand in silhouette there would be but to ask for trouble, for he would make a very tempting shot.

He turned to the left and moved deliberately until he was a good fifty yards along; then, however, he whipped off his burnous, and, rolling it up, jammed it down between some stones. Next he took out a pair of heavy automatic pistols, and with one in each hand started to run. He kept a sharp eye as he went along for signs of Berbers, but saw none until he had reached the very head of the wadi. Then he caught a brief glimpse of a motionless figure on a horse.

A man seemed to be gazing his way, but before Plummer could make sure he had wheeled and disappeared. It began to look as if there might be trouble from that direction as well, and with this fear in his mind Plummer was more anxious than ever to settle this disaffection among his own men.

At the head of the ravine he turned again to the left, made difficult progress over some stony ground, and then to the left again he reached the other side of the ravine.

Now he ran more quickly, for there was a goat track which had been beaten hard. As he drew near that side of the camp he paused once and listened. There seemed to be a confused murmur of voices coming from the direction of the camp, and suddenly he heard a shot. Abdul had been right there was mutiny afoot!

He broke into a run again, and when he was opposite the camp tore down the slope of the wadi at reckless speed. The shots had become sharp and rapid now, and some little distance before he reached the camp circle he could see a confused mass of men running in every direction, shooting as they went.

He jerked out his long-bladed knife as he ran, placing it between his teeth; then, with each pistol levelled he broke into the camp like a fury, shooting rapidly as he came.

There was an immediate cessation as all eyes turned to the wild-looking figure that dashed among them. In that pause Plummer sent three of them down, never to rise again, and a fourth crawled away with a smashed hip. On one side were his own men, faithful, as he had calculated; opposite them and near the precious treasure chest were Vali's men. They had struck, as he thought, the minute his back was turned.

Little had they counted on him returning thus. And before they could rally, Plummer was in the centre, standing straight and savage, as men had seen Sakr-el-Droog face the Spaniards and French, and now he shot slowly. His own men came back into action with loud yells, and charged.

Plummer held his fire then. He did not want to lose more men than was absolutely necessary, for he needed them on the march. And when his own men, among whom none was more valiant than little Abdul, had finished that dash through, the mutineers threw down their rifles and cried for quarter.

That was all Plummer wanted. He was among them swiftly and, getting them in a mass, talked to them in a way that froze them with fear. Sakr-el-Droog could put the fear of Allah in them when he wished. And well was it he had acted when he did, for scarcely had he reduced them to obedience than the whole place rang with yells. The Berbers were rushing them. They had seen the dissension in the camp, and, as Plummer had feared, chose that moment to strike.

For their own sakes the mutineers had to put up a defence. There was no quarter with these foes, and they knew it. And it was in that crisis that George Marsden Plummer showed at his best. He hadn't a shred of physical cowardice in him. It was his supreme disdain of danger that had lifted him high among men who courted death because it was a sure way to paradise and the lovely houris that Allah promised the Faithful. He revealed then why he had been called the Hawk of the Peak, and it was the name of Sakr-el-Droog that his men took up as their battle cry.

"Sakr-el-Droog!—Il-Allah — akbah Allah! Sakr-el-Droog!"

The din was appalling. There was a cloud of dust over everything, and even at close quarters every man was using his rifle. The Berbers had the advantage at first, for, on their wiry mountain horses, they had swept down the side of the wadi at a pace that carried them into and clean through the camp before they drew up.

But by the time they wheeled and were ready to return Plummer had rallied his men and, standing out in front of them was shooting with each hand as coolly as if he were potting bottles from the deck of a ship.

And then, on the very moment when the Berbers were on the pivot of the wheeling movement, he started forward, yelling the same name as he went. Mutineers and his own men were all out for him now, and as that dread name reached them above the din—as they realised they had attacked not a fat Fezzi merchant's caravan, but that of the fighting devil known as Sakr-el-Droog, the Berbers hesitated.

Plummer kept right on until he was in among them. Man after man he dropped from his saddle, and then, as he emptied both weapons, dropped them and caught hold of his knife, there was a loud command from the Berber leader. Another sharp wheeling motion followed, bringing them round and away like a flash. Up the other side of the wadi the horses scrambled; there was a pause at the top while a last volley was sent into the camp; then the troop disappeared in a heavy cloud of dust that settled in the camp like a hail of grit.

The mutiny had been squelched; the raid was over.

Two weeks later George Marsden Plummer was safely installed in Vali Mata-Vali's house at St. Cloud on the outskirts of Paris.

CHAPTER 5.   The Mystery of the House on the Creek—Three Dead Men—Sexton Blake Assists Scotland Yard.

POLICE-CONSTABLE TARRANT paused as he reached the top of the hill overlooking the village, and gazed across the valley to the east, where the first faint grey of summer dawn was just beginning to show. Lying at his feet was the little village still wrapped in slumber, and, beyond, the rolling downs.

For five minutes or so the constable stood drinking in the freshness of the morning; then he turned to continue his patrol. At that moment, however, his gaze encountered something that made him pause a second time. He walked to the side of the road and stood peering across the river flats in a puzzled way.

"That's funny," he muttered. "I didn't hear that there was a party at that place last night; but perhaps it isn't that—maybe someone is ill. I'll go along in that direction."

He retraced his steps for about twenty yards until he came to a stile. Climbing this, he followed a path that led down the slope of the hill to another stile; and when he had climbed that he plunged at once down a steep descent that led to the bank of the river.

A little distance along there was a boat tied to a tree, and, appropriating this craft, the constable pulled himself across to the other bank. He secured the boat there and again proceeded on foot until he reached a small creek which emptied into the river. He followed this until he came to a fence spanning the creek, and here he paused once more to survey the house which was now some three hundred yards distant.

Several times each day Police-constable Tarrant saw that house during his patrol—sometimes from one side of the valley, sometimes from the other, for it stood bleak and alone, visible from almost every point of the adjacent roads which intersected the constable's area.

But never before had it appeared as it did on this morning. On many an occasion he had noticed the glow of light against the blinds of one room or another—a perfectly usual sight. Now, however, every window in the place that was visible from where he stood was an illuminated oblong, and, as he moved still closer, bringing some of the side windows within his angle of vision, he saw that they showed up the same.

There was no reason why the occupant of the house shouldn't

burn his light all night if he took a fancy that way, but it was decidedly out of the usual run of conditions which the constable met with in his area, and curiosity led him on still further.

He knew little more about the man who lived there than what village gossip had told him. The individual in question was a Mr. John Dean, who had come to the district a year or so before, had bought the house on the creek and had gone into residence almost immediately.

There was only one manservant whom he had brought down from London with him, and this man was as retiring and close-mouthed as his master. One thing the constable was sure of, and that was that no entertaining ever took place there. Then why was every room illuminated at this hour of the morning?

He was quite certain the house had not presented that appearance in the neighbourhood of midnight when he had last passed that way.

He approached the front path and opened the gate. After hesitating a few moments he came to a decision. He would just see if all was as it should be. Striding up the path, he mounted the porch and was in the act of reaching up for the knocker when he noticed to his surprise, that the door was slightly ajar.

He knocked once and twice and thrice, but not a sound came in answer. He pushed the door open tentatively, stepped inside, and then he paused. Twice he opened his mouth as if he would call, and twice he hesitated. It was as if some invisible force restrained him from shattering the silence of the place—a silence that was uncanny under that hard, white electric light.

It was beginning to affect the constable, for, as a vagrant current of air caused the front door to thud softly against the wall, he turned sharply, nervously. Then, suddenly, he pulled himself together and rapped with his knuckles on the banisters, calling at the same time:

"Is there anyone at home?"

The sound of his own voice echoing in the regions above was the only answer, and now, determined to use his authority, he strode across the hall to the first door on his left. He knocked on this, then turned the handle and entered. He found himself in a large, well-furnished drawing-room, where every bulb in the central chandelier had been turned on; but of any human being there was no sign.

After a brief survey the constable retired and made his way along to the next door on that side of the hall. No summons to enter greeted his knock here, so again he took the initiative, finding himself in a cosy dining-room, where the lights were reflected from the polished top of a big mahogany table. On the sideboard masses of silver plate gleamed brightly, and so far as the constable could see, everything was in perfect order.

More baffled than ever, he closed the door and crossed the hall to the third. Again he tapped, then he entered a well-furnished study. Just over the threshold he drew up with a jerk, then he hastened forward and dropped to his knees beside the huddled form of a man who lay beside the overturned chair by the desk.

Police-constable Tarrant had not had much experience of violent death, but he had seen sufficient to know the meaning of the small hole which, as he turned the body over, he noticed in the exact centre of the forehead.

He got to his feet and stood looking about him. There was no sign of a weapon on the floor or the desk, and almost mechanically the constable found himself muttering:

"It's murder, that's what it is— murder! And it hasn't been so long ago either, for the body is still warm. I'll have to report this to the inspector at Arundel. But I'd better search the other rooms first."

He turned and made for the door, passing along the hall to the remaining room there which he had not yet examined. He swung the door open and peered in. It was a small breakfast-room, brilliantly lighted like the others, but revealing no sign of any human occupant.

The constable switched out the lights and closed the door. Then, keeping a wary eye ahead of him, he mounted the stairs. There were six bed-rooms on that floor, each of which he examined, but without result. He kept switching out the lights as he went along, and thinking to himself that he would have a look at the kitchen while he was about it, he started down the back staircase.

And, there at the bottom he got his second shock, for he came upon a huddled form lying against the door which led into the kitchen.

The constable dragged the body away and opened the door. He then lifted the body inside and began an examination. Dead he was right enough, but there was no sign of bullet or knife wound that the constable could see.

"This is the servant," he muttered. "And from what I have heard there was only this one to look after the place. How he died I don't know, but there has been a terrible business here during the night, and

I'd better lose no time in getting through to the inspector. Better leave them both just as they are until he comes."

He jumped up and hurried from the kitchen along the short hall which led to the dining-room, switching out the lights there as he passed through. He turned off the switch in the hall and other downstairs rooms before departing, and finding a key on the inside of the front door, he locked the place and took the key with him. His shortest way to the village and the nearest telephone was as he had come, and as he got outside the front gate he broke into a run.

Down the bank of the creek he raced and across the river flat to where he had left the boat tied. A couple of pulls at the oars sent him across, and hastily tying the painter to a tree there, he began the stiff climb up the path which led to the top of the chalk cliff.

It was broad day by now. As he descended into the village he saw smoke rising from the chimneys of almost every cottage, and on reaching the inn he found the door already ajar. The innkeeper, clad only in a shirt and trousers, was in the bar cleaning up the debris from the previous evening.

He was not surprised to see the constable at that hour of the morning, for he knew, as did all the village, that Tarrant had a habit of prowling about at all sorts of odd hours. But he did feel curious at the constable's obvious agitation, and still more so when he abruptly demanded the use of the telephone.

"What's up?" drawled the innkeeper in his slow way, as he took the other along to the parlour where the telephone was installed. "'Beant nothin' wrong, I hope?"

"I can't tell you anything now," jerked the constable. "And if you hear what I say over the telephone, don't you pass it on to anyone—not until after the inspector gets here from Arundel."

And then the innkeeper listened with dropped jaw and goggling eyes to what the constable had to say when, after a considerable delay, he finally got through to the inspector.

It was a coincidence that at the same time that Constable Tarrant was telephoning, the night patrol of the London River Police was fishing out of the Thames the limp body of a man.

• • • •

"There is a queer bit of business down in Sussex," remarked Inspector Thomas, as he absent-mindedly helped himself to one of Blake's cigars. "I thought perhaps you and Tinker might like to run down. If we start soon we could lunch at Horsham on the way."

"What is it?" asked Blake.

"I don't just know. We've had a message from the inspector at Arundel asking us to lend a hand. The bare facts of the case are that early this morning the local constable at a village near Arundel made a somewhat gruesome discovery in an isolated house on the river flats there. His attention was attracted to the place by the fact that, as dawn was breaking, every window in the house was illuminated. He thought it rather queer, and went across to investigate. On entering the house he found two dead men, the master and the servant. There are certain features about it which appear to be extremely puzzling, and, according to the Arundel Inspector, it would seem to be murder single, if not double. Unlike a good many of those birds in the country, the Arundel inspector knows the value of the machinery which Scotland Yard can bring into place so he has asked our aid."

"I think I should like to go down with you," remarked Blake. "We can take the Grey Panther, if you wish."

"All right, it's all the same to me, but I have one visit to make before we go. I want to drop in at the morgue to have a look at a body that was fished out of the river last night."

"A case of suicide?"

"It seems to be."

"Well, we can drive along there first, and then go straight on."

"All right."

Blake turned to Tinker.

"Go round and get the car, will you? See that the tanks are in order."

Ten minutes later, Tinker at the wheel, they drove away, making first for that dismal, gruesome place known as the morgue. Arriving there, Blake and Tinker accompanied the inspector inside, and stood beside him while he made an examination of the poor wretch who had been fished out of the river that morning.

The divisional police-surgeon's report would make it appear that it was a case of ordinary suicide, and certainly, from the ragged condition of the few greasy garments in which the man had been clad, one could easily imagine that he was just one of those human derelicts who had reached his limit.

The only mark in the form of a bruise was on the side of the head, just above the left ear, and this might well have been caused by the head coming into contact with something when the wretch threw himself in. There appeared to be nothing whatsoever to assist the police in learning his identity.

The clothes were the mixed assortment of any tramp, and if they had ever borne any maker's label the marks had been removed. The pockets had revealed nothing except a few trivial odds and ends and just a half-penny in money, nor did there appear to be any distinctive marks of identification on the body, with the exception of one small patch on the throat, as large, perhaps, as a half-crown, which stood up even whiter than the rest of the pallid skin.

To Blake's scrutiny it looked as if at some time or other the man had suffered a wound or operation there, and that it had been necessary to graft on fresh skin. On the other hand, it might have been just an ordinary patch such as a birthmark.

Like the inspector, however, Blake did not attach any particular importance to the find. It was frequent enough that the body of some human derelict was fished out of the Thames, and it was frequent enough, too, that they were buried in an unmarked grave, for there is no one to take very much interest in such unfortunate wretches. He agreed with Thomas that, to his knowledge, he had never seen the man before, and when the inspector had given certain directions for a search to be made among the records of Scotland Yard, to see if the man had ever passed through their hands, they re-entered the car and started on their drive into Sussex.

Inspector Thomas had made a rendezvous at the little inn in the village at Houghton, and when they arrived there in the early afternoon, after having lunched at Horsham, they found the Arundel inspector, Morrow, and two of his men waiting for them.

"I'm glad you came as well, Mr. Blake," he said, as he shook hands. "This is the sort of case you ought to find interesting. We can drive over the bridge and reach the house in that way."

He joined them in the Grey Panther and instructed his two men to cut across the flats on foot. Then Tinker turned, and, driving back the way they had come, crossed the bridge, picking up the road on the right which would take them to what Inspector Morrow referred to as the house on the creek.

He told Thomas and Blake what he could as they went along, and by the time Tinker drew up in front of the gates they had gathered the following:

It appeared that the occupant of the house on the creek had not lived there for long; a matter of a year or so. It was not known exactly where he had come from, but it was believed that he had lived for many years in Canada. During his occupancy of the house on the creek the residents round about were equally as vague about his habits of life, for he had not encouraged visitors— in fact, he had lived a life of rigid seclusion, attended only by a single manservant.

It was believed that he had been well-to-do, for he had bought the house on the creek, together with a hundred acres of land adjoining it, lock, stock and barrel, for something in the neighbourhood of thirteen thousand pounds spot cash.

This much was known, but little more, and certainly, from the mode of life he had led, it could not have been the giving of any entertainment which could account for the constable having seen every room in the place illuminated as the summer dawn was breaking.

So much Inspector Morrow was able to tell them by the time Tinker came to a stop.

"Dr. Ross is still here," he remarked, as they passed a two-seater car drawn up by the fence. "I have told him to leave everything as nearly as possible as they were when the local constable made the discovery. He probably has finished his examination by now. We shall hear what he has to say."

They entered the house, and passed down the hall to the study where Constable Tarrant had made his first discovery. The body had been lifted on to a couch, and a clean-shaven, professional-looking man was standing beside it writing in a note-book. Inspector Morrow introduced him as the doctor, who shot a look of interest at Blake when he heard his name.

"What is the result?" asked Morrow.

"I should say that death was certainly instantaneous," was the answer.

"I shall make a detailed statement at the inquest, but, as far as I can learn at present, death was caused by a bullet of small calibre fired at close range, but, not so close as to blacken the skin."

"We have found no weapons so far," remarked Inspector Morrow, turning to Blake and Thomas. "He was lying here on the floor beside this chair. He must have been seated at the desk writing when someone entered the room. My theory is that he turned to speak to this person, and it was then the shot was fired. At any rate, the chair was overturned, just as if he had lurched to one side and upset it as he fell to the floor. Does that fit in with what you have discovered, doctor?"

"Perfectly. It was not a very powerful weapon, or the bullet would have come out at some other part of the skull. A post-mortem will probably show that it is embedded in the brain, near the back wall of the skull, but whoever did fire the shot was an expert in the use of such a weapon."

"What about the servant?" put in Thomas. "Inspector Morrow tells us that he was found dead at the foot of the back stairs."

"Yes. I have had him carried in and placed on a couch in the dining-room. He died from a broken neck, but whether he fell down the stairs, or was thrown down, I am not prepared to say."

"Have you come upon anything that would seem to indicate a clue?" ventured Blake, who had been listening closely.

Inspector Morrow shook his head. "Nothing so far, but I have not had time to make a detailed examination. The local constable assures me that he left everything just as he found it, and, beyond noticing that this top left-hand drawer in the desk was open, as you see it now, nothing appears to have been disturbed. But that, of course, is difficult to say, for we have no means of knowing just what was here."

"He might have pulled that drawer out himself," put in Thomas. "It is a natural enough thing to do when one is sitting at a desk writing. What was he writing, at any rate? What was on the desk?"

"That is the odd thing about it," rejoined Morrow. "There were no written sheets on the blotting-pad. It may have been that he was just about to begin, or was—"

"Or the murderer took what he had been writing," supplemented Thomas.

"Yes—exactly."

"Have you knowledge of any friends or relatives?" asked Blake.

Morrow shook his head.

"No. But I've found a bank book, and I have sent a telegram to London. His banker there may be able to give us some information."

"What I can't understand is why the lights should be turned on in every room," remarked Thomas, rubbing his chin. "Why should he want to do that? What reason do you think he could have had, Blake?"

Blake shrugged.

"One might venture several guesses. It was not habitual with him, or I take it the local constable would have noticed it before. Therefore, if we assume that last night was the first occasion on which he had done this, then he must have had some strong motive. I have seen something of a similar nature in the past, and I have found that usually it is through fear. It is possible that he knew death was threatening him, and illuminating every room was one of the precautions he took."

"Um, there might be something in that," muttered Thomas. "But it certainly is a queer business. What time would you say death took place, doctor?"

"My opinion is that he was alive at three o'clock this morning, and that he was killed some time between then and when the constable found him."

"And what about the manservant?"

"I should say his death occurred shortly before or after that of his master."

"Yet they were both fully dressed at that hour of the morning," murmured Blake. "It would almost look as if some danger had been anticipated."

"If some threat had been made against his life, why didn't he notify the police, I wonder?" said Morrow.

"He may have had strong personal reasons for not doing so," rejoined Blake. "We don't know what secret there was in his life. By the way, what was his name?"

"Dean—John Dean."

"If some record of his life can be traced we might get light on that," proceeded Blake.

Blake was about to say something else, when there came a knock on the door, and one of Inspector Morrow's men entered. He approached his chief and said something in a low tone. Morrow looked up in surprise at what he heard. Then he turned to Blake and Thomas.

"A man had just arrived from London by the afternoon train," he said in a low tone. "He gives his name as Henry Dean, and states that he is a cousin of John Dean. He asks what the police are doing on the premises, and demands to see his cousin."

CHAPTER 6. What Did Henry Dean Know?—Sexton Blake Makes an Important Discovery.

NEITHER Blake nor Thomas had time to make a reply before there was a scuffling sound outside the door, then a voice raised in impatient protest. The next moment the door was thrown open, and a bearded man of big frame pushed his way into the room with a constable still clinging to his arm.

"I have a perfect right to enter, and I intend doing so," he was saying. "I'm going to know the meaning of all this. It has taken me long enough to find my cousin. If there are any objections I'll hear them afterwards, and—good heavens, what is the meaning of this?"

It was just then that his eyes fell on the stiff form on the couch, and, ignoring the four men by the desk, he threw off the constable and strode forward, bending down to peer at the face of the dead man.

"John—John Dean, my cousin!"

Then he straightened up and turned to the group.

"What does this mean," he demanded harshly, "and who are you gentlemen?"

It was Inspector Morrow who made reply.

"I am the police-inspector from Arundel," he said curtly. "This gentleman"—and he indicated Thomas —"is an inspector from Scotland Yard; this"—indicating Blake—"is a friend of his, and this is a doctor acting on behalf of the police. Now, sir, perhaps you'll be good enough to tell me who you are?"

The stranger looked at them one after the other, then he passed a bewildered hand across his forehead.

"I am Henry Dean," he managed to say at last. "This is my cousin, whose whereabouts I have been seeking since I arrived in England a week ago. It is only to-day that I learnt where he was living, and I left London at once. But what has happened? What does it mean?"

Inspector Morrow glanced towards Thomas, who replied with a faint nod:

"As far as we can discover, your cousin has been murdered during the night," answered Morrow. "His servant seems to have met a similar fate. That is all we can tell you so far. But your coming is opportune, for perhaps you can enlighten us regarding his life before he came here."

"I am afraid I can't help you much there," was the answer. "It is more than twenty years since I saw him last, and I know practically nothing of his life during those years. All I know is what I have learnt from a solitary letter which he wrote me some months ago, saying that he had arrived in England and intended settling here. I myself reached England just a week ago, and until to-day his bank refused to give me his address.

"I wrote him two letters through them, which I presume he received, and I had one in reply two days ago, telling me that he was not in a position at the moment to entertain me, but would communicate with me at an early date, as he wished me to come and stay with him. I was puzzled over this, for I was anxious to see him, and I could not understand why he should put me off. But to-day I was called up on the telephone from his bank and given the address, with the suggestion that I should, if possible, travel down to-day."

His listeners were one and all thinking that what inspired the telephone message from the bank was possibly the telegram which Inspector Morrow had sent that morning—that the bank manager, fearing something was wrong, although Morrow had worded it ambiguously, had taken it upon himself to reveal the address to the cousin in London. It all seemed to dovetail well enough, at any rate.

"Then until to-day you did not know where he was living?" answered Morrow.

"Not in the least. But you have said, inspector, that he has been killed —murdered. What does it mean? Who has done this dastardly thing?"

"That is just what we are extremely anxious to find out," rapped Morrow. "Have you no knowledge whatsoever of any enemy whom your cousin might have had?"

"None. As I have told you, I have been out of touch with him for many years. We were always the best of friends, and I could not understand why he would not reveal his address on my arrival in England. In a letter which I had from him a few days ago he seemed most anxious to renew our old acquaintance, and I took it that private business of some sort was the reason he was postponing our meeting. He used to be a bit odd about his movements, and I came to the conclusion that he hadn't changed."

"Can you tell me if he was married?"

"Not to my knowledge. As far as I know, I am his sole living relative."

Morrow looked perplexed. The stranger's statement seemed perfectly above board, yet he could not but think it was a little odd that he should arrive at such a moment. He felt that he would like to discuss this new phase of the matter alone with Blake and Thomas, and yet he did not want to lose the new arrival as a valuable witness. Blake was reading his thoughts, and, unseen by the others, he gave Inspector Thomas a nudge which stirred the man from Scotland Yard into action.

"It is a little too soon to go into this phase of the matter, I think," remarked Thomas, "but we shall wish to have your evidence at the inquest Mr. Dean, and it would be as well, perhaps, if you could remain in the district until that is over."

Thomas did not explain that he would take good care to see that this stranger was not lost sight of, but all the others, as well as Blake and Tinker, knew that was what he meant.

If he expected the other to show any signs of disinclination he was mistaken. The man who called himself Henry Dean nodded an immediate agreement.

"I'll stay down here, of course. As a matter of fact, I'm quite willing; to remain in the house, and, as his next-of-kin I think I should. I don't know what you do in a case like this, but if you prefer that I should go to a local inn, I shall do so."

Nothing could have been more open or evident of a desire to fit in with police arrangements than that. Thomas glanced at Morrow, and then his gaze went to Blake. Blake gave the merest of nods hoping that the man from Scotland Yard would interpret it correctly; and he did.

"As you have come prepared to remain, I think you may as well stay in the house," rejoined Thomas "Before the inquest, I hope we shall discover more about your cousin, who appears to have been a man of few friends down here. We shall be glad of any help you can give us."

"Certainly—anything in my power!" answered the other. Then he turned once more to gaze at the figure on the couch.

"I wonder—" he began, as if to himself.

"Yes?" put in Thomas when his voice trailed off.

"I was wondering if his letters to me asking me to come down had anything to do with the cause of his death. He seemed anxious for me to visit him, and yet, as I have told you, he seemed to want to put it off for the immediate present."

"Have you kept those letters?"

"Oh, yes! They are in my bag."

"You will probably be asked to produce them."

"I shall do so, of course. You are welcome to see them whenever you wish."

"Then I shall ask you to wait in another room until our examination is complete—not in the dining-room please. There has been a second tragedy."

"A second tragedy! Do you mean—"

"Your cousin lived here with a single manservant. He also has been found dead."

"My cousin mentioned in one of his letters that he was living very quietly with one servant. Do you mean the man has been murdered?"

"We are not in a position to make a statement about it yet."

The stranger looked more bewildered than ever, but had sense enough to see that the inspector did no wish to prolong the conversation just then. So muttering something about waiting in some other room, he passed out. As soon as he was gone, Thomas spoke to Morrow and the latter signalled to one of his men to keep an eye on Henry Dean. Then a suggestion was made that they should move along to the dining-room to have a look at the servant's body.

Up to this moment Sexton Blake had only been a spectator. The only active part he had taken in the proceedings was to pass an opinion— very cautiously worded—when he was asked a question, and to send a look to Thomas indicating that the stranger should be allowed to take up his quarters in the house.

But now he lagged behind when the others moved towards the door. He had not made any examination of the body in this room, and he had seen that Thomas' scrutiny had been only of a superficial nature, the man from the Yard having concerned himself more directly with the doctor's report.

"I'll just have a look here, and come along in a few moments," was all Blake said.

Tinker remained with him, watching while his master made a close examination of the wound in the centre of the forehead, and then extended his scrutiny to the body. He worked quickly and efficiently, for the work was of a sort to which he was well accustomed. When he had finished he straightened up and glanced at his assistant.

"Come on, Tinker; we'll join the others."

"Find anything in particular, guv'nor?"

"Um! I should say that the doctor's opinion about sums it up," was Blake's reply.

And Tinker gave it no more thought. What he would have said had he known that Blake had found something worthy of acute interest might have been very different.

In the dining-room they stood near the end of the couch while the police surgeon demonstrated simply how the man had met his death.

"The vertebrae of the neck are twisted and broken in two places," he said, laying his fingers on the spot. "Death was instantaneous, as in the case of his master, but whether it was by accident or not I cannot pass an opinion."

As he straightened up, and Thomas and Morrow began to discuss the question of a weapon, deciding to lose no time in making a thorough search of the house and a careful examination of all letters and other documents, Blake sauntered close to the couch and bent over the corpse. The servant was a man somewhere in the neighbourhood of fifty. He was a little over medium height, rather stoutish, and Blake noticed that his skin was of a wind-and-sun-beaten texture, such as one seldom finds among indoor servants. He was clean-shaven, with the exception of greyish "sideboards," cut close. The latter were the only things about him that stamped him as a servant.

Blake could see that, without those bits of side whisker, he would have had more the appearance of a seafaring-man, or, at least, of one who had lived most of his years in the open air. He was in marked physical contrast to his dead master, who had been thin and of small frame.

Blake did not pursue his examination long. He pressed the snapped vertebrae tentatively with his fingers, and lifted each lid for a look at the eyes; then he straightened up and turned to listen to what the two inspectors were saying. They were just on the point of starting their search of the house, a job at which he and Tinker lent a hand.

They soon found that, with the exception of the study where John Dean had been killed, and some drawers in the main bed-room, which it was plain had been used by him, there was practically nothing to hold their attention. As a matter of fact, the contents of most of the rooms had been left just as they were when the dead man had taken over the place, and almost all the apartments had that indefinable air of not having been lived in for some time.

Nor did the servant's bed-room reveal anything to hold their attention except one object. That was a long stockwhip, fully twelve feet from the butt of its short handle to the end of the knotted lash, which hung on the wall of the room.

It was a curious souvenir to find such a place, and it was plain that at some time or other it had been used considerably. It was marked down as an item to be taken into consideration, but was not removed from its place.

The study revealed nothing which could seem to throw any light on the mystery. There were letters from the bank to which the inspector had telegraphed, some tradesmen's bills (some receipted), a fire insurance policy covering the house and its contents, some pencilled figures on a block of paper, a plain card on which had been written the name of Henry Dean, and beneath that the address of a London hotel, and in the upper right-hand desk a couple of walnuts, dark as mahogany and highly polished from much rubbing. At first glance Sexton Blake recognised them as the sort of nuts used by high caste Chinese gentlemen for rolling round and round against each other in the hand as a means to concentration on some portion of the Five Classics, or in religious contemplation.

Of the usual collection of papers, letters, and what-not which the average person gathers about him, there was not a sign. The dead man must have been of an extraordinary neat and tidy nature, or else he had deliberately kept the place stripped of every shred of superfluous writing. Nor was there any safe to be seen where he might have locked away documents.

There was a small compartment the desk which, on being opened with one of the keys on a bunch taken from the dead man's pocket, revealed packet of notes such as might have been kept for current expenses. There was also a cheque-book and a second bank pass-book, which had been completely filled up. That was about all they came upon.

It was almost as bare as it might have been if the man had met his death in a hotel room, which he was occupying temporarily, instead of the study where, presumably, he worked or read every day and every evening. The bookcases were well filled, and most of the volumes showed signs of plenty of handling, but whether that had been by the dead man, or those who had owned the volumes previously, was not evident then.

By the time the search of the house was completed, the affair was as much of a mystery as ever. No sign of pistol had been found. Whoever had killed John Dean had taken the weapon away with him. If it had been the servant who had committed the murder which was a theory that had to be considered, although it did not seem probable— then he had got rid of the weapon in some way before falling to his own death down the secondary staircase.

There were plenty of signs, however, which made it look as if the murderer had come from outside, and not only that, but had been expected. Such a theory seemed the most reasonable to explain why all the lights were on. John Dean had feared death, and, like so many persons who are filled with dread, had felt he stood a better chance by steeping himself in light. But that brilliance had not saved him.

Who had come to the house during the night? How had he reached it? Had he come by road—by motor! Or had he been lying low for some hours, perhaps for days, waiting an opportunity? Was it this fear which had impelled John Dean to put off seeing his cousin? Or had his mind worked the other way? Had he intended having his cousin with him because he thought he was in danger, and had he been struck down before he had had a chance to complete his arrangements?

There were scores of questions to mull over, and Thomas took occasion to do so as they drove back to London. Blake listened to what he said, putting in a remark now and then, but not committing himself to anything definite. For Sexton Blake had not only seen something about the dead body of John Dean to rouse his acute interest; he had found the same condition when examining the servant.

And that was a round, white mark on the side of the neck—a mark about the size of a half-crown—exactly similar to that which he had noticed on the throat skin of the man who had been fished out of the Thames the previous night.

CHAPTER 7.   The House of the High-caste Chinaman—The Sign of the Tong.

MR. HONG-LO-SOO the wealthy and influential Chinese merchant of Packers Court, Limehouse, was in a very perturbed state of mind. There was nothing about that smooth, round, fat visage to reveal this; but those who were nearest to that amiable gentleman's confidence, would have been able to perceive his agitated state of mind from the unceasing rapidity with which he rolled two highly polished walnuts together in his right hand.

Round and round and round they went, grinding and rubbing together in a way that only occurred when Hong-Lo-Soo was much upset over something. Nearly always he carried the walnuts —as do most Chinese gentlemen—and nearly always he was rubbing them together. But usually that motion was a slow one, which was soothing to the mind and conductive to pleasant reminiscence.

But on this day the spirit of vicious impatience seemed to have entered into the Celestial's hand, so rapidly did it move.

Ever since the hour of morning rice, Hong-Lo-Soo had been giving audience in his private room at the back of his extensive premises in Packers Court.

In the front part of the building everything was the same as any other European place of business. The clerks, although Chinese, were dressed in garments of the West, and the large warehouse was piled in orthodox fashion with great tiers of chests containing tea, bales of choice Shantung silks, boxes of camphor from Formosa, sacks of unpolished rice for his own race, and well-padded crates containing specimens of very choice lacquer.

It was a place of pungent, alluring odours of that warehouse, for in it was something of almost every product of the East. Hong-Lo-Soo's business was of a most catholic nature, for its branches encircled the globe, and he either imported against cash, or exchanged in kind, the raw produce of the whole vast East.

Each interview which he had granted had left him in a more perturbed state than ever. Some of his visitors had been old, and some young; some poor and shabbily clad, and some wealthy merchants of his own standing. But all had been Chinese, and each one had given a certain tong sign on entering, which meant that they were tong brothers of Hong-Lo-Soo.

As a matter of fact, a certain portion of Chinatown in London was seething with suppressed excitement. This section was made up of all who belonged to the influential Four Lakes Tong or its affiliated brotherhood, the Three Feathers Tong. A certain whisper had become most persistent, and if it should prove to be true, then it meant a most unthinkable calamity.

As the most powerful Celestial in both tongs, and even among his own race in London, it was to Hong-Lo-Soo that the various messengers came. Into his attentive ear was murmured report after report, but only in the steadily increasing rate of whirling the two walnuts in his hand did Hong-Lo-Soo reveal the effect the different items of information were having upon him.

For more than an hour he had been sitting cross-legged on some cushions, looking not unlike a stout, silken-clad Buddha. He had given orders that he was not to be intruded upon until he rang his silver bell, and when he did finally stretch out his hand to lift it, his words were not an instruction to admit other visitors.

On the contrary. He informed the "boy" who entered that he was at home to no one, and then, rising, he pushed aside a matting panel in the wall which admitted him at once to the main household apartments.

Half an hour later Mr. Hong-Lo-Soo emerged from the front entrance of his business place in Packers Court dressed as a European. He was wearing a well-cut morning coat, lavender-striped trousers, and well-brushed silk hat. He carried a pair of pale grey gloves and a very handsome malacca stick. At the kerb stood a most luxurious Rolls-Royce car with driver and footman in attendance, both uniformed in the shade of deep plum which Hong-Lo-Soo favoured.

The footman stood respectfully by the open door until his honourable master entered, then he waited obsequiously while the merchant gave instructions where he wished to be driven.

The destination he named was a house in Baker Street, and, indeed, the moment Hong-Lo-Soo had appeared, every clerk in his establishment knew that the master was bound for the West End of London on some important call, for when Hong-Lo-Soo did pay a formal visit he did it in the full pomp due to his rank and station.

It was perhaps forty minutes later that the merchant was shown into Sexton Blake's consulting-room. His visits to Blake were of rare occurrence, but when he did come he was certain of a very friendly reception, for the mandarin and the criminologist were very old and well-tried friends.

Indeed, on a certain occasion in the past, Blake had not only become a member of the Four Lakes and the Three Feathers tongs, but he had initiated as a full blood-brother in the former, a thing that could happen to a European only under very exceptional circumstances.

Tinker, who had no little respect and awe for Hong-Lo-Soo despite his race, was ready to place a chair for him close to Blake's desk, and with his usual punctilious courtesy, the Celestial acknowledged it after he had greeted Blake. He spoke perfect English, and, with the difference that his manners were almost too correct, acted as a Westerner when he was among them. Hong-Lo-Soo was a very high-caste gentleman, and fully cultured, as he should be, for he was a deep scholar of the Five Classics, than which there is no more complete treatise on the whole duty of man.

He accepted one of Blake's choice sobranie cigarettes, and for the occasion of his visit had left his walnuts behind. Therefore he was free to gesture with both hands as well as arms, which he found necessary when conversing in English. And scarcely had he begun to speak than Sexton Blake knew he had come on no ordinary courtesy visit.

Had Hong-Lo-Soo been receiving Blake in his own private apartment, where his surroundings and dress were of his country, he would have indulged in the flowery compliments which form such an important code of formality among the Chinese. But here in this consulting-room he spoke as straight to the point as any Western business man

"I am come to consult you, my friend, on a matter of the utmost importance. In the past, on many occasions, you have lent your aid to me and to the tongs to which we both have the honour to belong. But never, old friend, have I had such a case as this to present to your wise mind. I am come because these things are taking place in the West, and here you can move swiftly, where I am handicapped."

"I am deeply grieved to know that something serious is amiss, dear friend. What is wrong?"

Hong-Lo-Soo bent forward until his august "seat of wisdom" (the abdomen) was seriously contracted. Had it not been for the gravity of the moment Tinker would have smiled. But he knew from the mandarin's words that something big was in the wind. And, knowing what had happened in the past when Blake had tackled cases for the Celestial, he was all ears to hear what it was. Nor was he unmindful of the fact that Hong-Lo-Soo was speaking in front of him with as much trust in his discretion as he had in Blake —or nearly so.

"You have heard of the Five Pearl Thimbles of Chen-tse. One night in Canton we conversed at length—you and the illustrious Hsui-fsi (Sir Gordon Saddler, the Mystery Man of 'Frisco), and my unworthy self. On that occasion we spoke of the Five Pearl Thimbles of Chen-tse."

Blake recalled the night perfectly. He remembered how Sir Gordon had related what he knew—which was all that anyone knew of those wonderful pearls. And it had been one of the greatest compliments ever paid to Sexton Blake, as he well knew.

"I remember, Hong-Lo-Soo."

"Those gems have been stolen, my friend."

The words were simple enough, but even the Celestial's control was hardly sufficient to keep the tremor out of his voice. It was to him a more portentous thing than if half of China had slipped into the sea, for this was desecration such as we of the West do not comprehend. It was a deadly insult to Buddha, who is of a sacredness profound to devout Celestials like Hong-Lo-Soo. And Blake knew it. His face was aghast at the news.

"The Five Pearl Thimbles of Chen-tse — stolen," he echoed. "Good heavens! Is your information correct?"

"Alas, it is only too true! There has been very evil work, my friend. But wait. Before I say more you must read."

He took a thick snake-skin wallet from an inside pocket and extracted a folded bit of paper, which proved to be a newspaper clipping. As soon as he opened it up Blake saw that it had been taken from a certain Paris paper of some weeks back. He read it slowly and carefully. It was, he found, a rather lurid description, after the style of French journalism (which leaves nothing to the imagination), of the finding of what was described as the caricature of a human being wandering about the Bois.

There was a revolting picture of the mental and physical condition of this thing that had come into the hands of the police, and farther down it was stated that, as near as could be ascertained, the man was Chinese. There was more—lots of it, but the gist was the same.

Blake looked up when he had finished.

"I read something of this in the English journals, but nothing with this sort of detail. I must have missed it in the French papers. What does it mean?"

"That was man of my race. In that much the article is correct. It was that man who stole the Five Pearl Thimbles of Chen-tse."

"Poor wretch—poor wretch. But I do not understand, Hong-lo-Soo. There was devil's work there."

"He deserved—worse," said the mandarin coldly. "But I agree that it never should have been carried out in Europe. It was a mistake. There were other means and places. But let me explain. That man was Prince Fu Won Chang of Manchuria."

"The name is familiar. Wasn't he at one time on the staff of the late Sun Yat Sen?"

"You are quite right. It was through that position he gained a certain entry to the Temple of Eternal Purity, in Canton. And that entry enabled him to reach the five pearls and steal them. I do not know how he did so; that may never be answered. But he did take them, and then fled to Europe. I cannot believe that the evil spirits of the dread Fen-Won were in him. He acted like a maniac. Hearken, my friend. Have you ever heard of a woman of the stage who has become well known in Paris—she is called in your tongue the Bird of Paradise?"

"I have heard of her, and I have seen her."

"Ah! She is very beautiful, I have heard."

"She is. She is, I fancy, a most extraordinarily fascinating creature. But where does she come into this?"

"Fu Won Chang saw her, and fell madly in love. He offered her all his possessions to become his wife, but she laughed at him. The man must have been filled with the evil spirits of Fen-Won, as I have said. He must have known that the priests of the temple would rest neither day or night until they found him. He must have realised that, when it became known every follower of Buddha would be seeking him. But he disregarded all this. In his evil passion he was worse than mad. He offered to this woman the Five Pearl Thimbles of Chen-tse."

"Truly, he must have been mad," muttered Blake, who knew what it meant.

"He had been found in Paris by the priests who had set out to trace him. They hovered over him night and day. They watched his every movement. In the very house of this woman they had paid spies among the servants. And thus did they know when he offered that terrible insult to the sacred Buddha. He left the woman to bring her the pearls. He started back to her, but he never reached her. On the way he was seized, and—and you have read what that paper says, my friend."

Blake nodded and frowned.

"I have read it, Hong-lo-Soo, but I cannot agree with the methods used by the priests. I realise to the full what a terrible desecration this man was guilty of, but that is no authority for destroying his soul. Buddha himself would not condone it."

For a few moments the Oriental and the Occidental eyed each other. Then Hong-Lo-Soo sighed.

"Twenty years ago I should have opposed your statement, but now I must agree with it. That is why I am here. Had I been informed in the beginning as I should have been informed, being the father of all senior tongs, then this would not have happened. I should have found the man —yes. And he should have been punished. But not in this way. I have come to know and to realise the sense of Western justice. Moreover, it was all a failure."

"In what way? Did they not find the pearls?"

"They recovered one only. Who can tell what is the truth? Did he possess the five sacred gems? Or did he have but one? Was he lying to the woman when he said he would bring her five? For the spies overheard his every word. Or did he bring but one to tempt her? He will never answer those questions now, for he will never speak again. That is where the priests over-reached themselves, as you would say, my friend. They were fools. They do this thing, and then when they find but one pearl it is too late to learn the truth. It is little satisfaction that this unmentionable creature has been turned loose with the mark of 'wei-len-pung' on his throat."

"The mark of wei-len-pung—wait, Hong-Lo-Soo, wait, I pray you."

The Celestial permitted himself to be mildly puzzled at the sudden agitation which had overwhelmed Sexton Blake. Tinker, too, could not fathom what had thrown Blake into such a state of excitement. They both watched him while he jumped up and began pacing up and down the room. Then he resumed his seat as abruptly as he had risen and drew a pad of plain paper towards him.

Picking up a pencil he began to sketch rapidly. Watching him, Hong-Lo-Soo could see that he was making a rough sketch of a human head and neck. And then, near the front of the neck, but a little to one side, he drew a circular line which he filled in with long, shading strokes.

"Look, please," he said when he had finished. "Let us imagine that this rough sketch I have made would be the colour of human skin. And let us say that this circular spot would be dead white in colour. Wouldn't that be similar to the mark of wei-len-pung?"

"That is so, my friend. You have seen the mark of wei-len-pung. Only one who had seen it could draw it and place it there."

"I have seen it. That was years ago in Chekiang. But I have seen it since then, Hong-Lo-Soo. I saw it only yesterday."

"By the sacred toe of the Buddha! Is this true, Mr. Blake?"

"True, true. I was dull, stupid not to think of the wei-len-pung before. But the mark of the religious outcast—of what we would call the lost soul never occurred to me. I was not thinking of your race or of the Buddhist religion. The mark of wei-len-pung. Good heavens! Don't you remember, Tinker?"

Tinker nodded quickly.

"You mean the marks you spoke of as being on the necks of those two men at the house near Arundel, guv'nor."

"Yes—yes. But that is not all. I have seen it on the necks of three men, Hong-Lo-Soo, and each man was a dead man."

For once the mandarin was jolted out of his Oriental calm. If what his English friend said was right, then he had seen, within a few hours, the mark of soul defilement which was known among the Chinese as "wei-len-pung." It was the worst brand that could be put on a man. It was set there after his mind and soul had been destroyed for all men to see and heed. It meant that a man so marked would never find repose among his sacred ancestors.

To the Chinese such a fate is exactly similar as would be the casting out of heaven of a Christian—only the Chinese take that factor more intensely than the Westerner can understand. The mark of "wei-len-pung" is worse than the mark of the "beast 666." It is eternal perdition of the most terrible kind.

"And you say you have seen this mark recently on the necks of three dead men—on the necks of three of my race?"

"No. It was branded on the skin of Europeans. But it was the same brand —the mark of 'wei-len-pung.' I am certain of it now. Good heavens! I wonder what it means. This is opening out, Hong-Lo-Soo."

"Please explain, my friend."

"I shall do so."

Then Blake began, and told briefly how he had gone down into the country with Detective-Inspector Thomas, of Scotland Yard, to investigate what looked like a double murder.

He told how, on the way, they had stopped at the morgue to look at the body of a man who had been found floating in the river the night before.

He had first noticed such a mark on that man's neck, and been struck by finding the same sort of dead white circle in the same place on the skin of the other two.

As a matter of fact, since his return to London the previous evening he had been deeply puzzled over the coincidence, and said so. But as he had not been definitely commissioned to investigate the case he had not followed up the matter farther.

Hong-Lo-Soo listened in an absorbed manner. When Blake had finished he drew out his watch.

"It is still early afternoon" he said slowly. "This man who was found in the river, my friend, would it be possible for us to see the body?"

"There would be no difficulty if it is still there."

"Would you do me the great honour to come in my poor vehicle?"

The choice of words showed that Hong-Lo-Soo was deeply moved.

"Of course I'll come," returned Blake, who was almost as moved as the other. "We shall go at once."

Thus it was that half an hour later, Sexton Blake and Tinker walked into that chill dread building accompanied by a stout Celestial dressed in the height of fashion. The official in charge gazed in astounded fashion at the apparition, but Blake was persona grata, and no difficulty was made about his seeing the body of the man who had been found in the river two nights before, and which still lay there.

They moved along to the cold slab where it lay. Bending down Blake gently drew back the covering, and then he moved a little to one side so that Hong-Lo-Soo could see clearly. The stout Celestial had his eyes fastened on the dead white mark that showed against the different white of the rest of the skin if such a differentiation can be permitted. Yet there was a difference, for the mark was plainly visible.

And then as Hong-Lo-Soo's lips began to move Blake and Tinker heard him whisper:

"You are right—it is the mark of 'wei-len-pung.' What can it mean?"

CHAPTER 8.   Investigations in Paris —Blake Tries a Queer Experiment.

TWO days after their visit to the morgue with Hong-Lo-Soo, Sexton Blake and Tinker sat at a small table in front of a certain little cafe which rests in the very shadow of Notre Dame in Paris.

Blake's decision to go to Paris may be summed up in exactly three words: "Find the woman."

He reached this point of deduction that was simple enough. On leaving the morgue he and Tinker had accompanied Hong-Lo-Soo to that gentleman's establishment in Packers Court. There, the Celestial had laid before Blake all the information in his possession, elaborating each point of special importance by sending for another of his race who could give Blake particulars in full detail.

By that evening Blake had acquired a fairly comprehensive history of the Five Pearl Thimbles of Chen-tse; and at the earnest solicitation of the merchant he had agreed to take up the case.

It was clear enough that the Manchu, Fu Won Chang, had braved the wrath of living priests and dead ancestors in order to steal the priceless gems. It may be explained here briefly just what was meant by the Five Pearl Thimbles of Chen-tse.

It has been the custom among the upper classes of the Chinese to permit the finger-nails to grow to a prodigious length. It is said that those of the late Queen Dowager were no less than four inches in length, but this may be something of an exaggeration. It was a badge of the class; it denoted that the person who could permit his nails to grow to this length had no need for "degrading" labour! A pretty fancy which could only be born in the Oriental mind.

There were, however, many risks of these long nails becoming broken by accidental contact with something and, therefore, finger-shields were necessary. These usually took the form of long, gold "thimbles"—there is no English word that exactly translates the Chinese word for those guards—but sometimes they were made of silver.

As centuries rolled by, they became a badge of great distinction, and hence symbolic. There is little doubt that the strange custom had its origin far back in the mists of time, and, certainly, the so-called Pearl Thimbles of Chen-tse, which were said to have been worn by the Buddha himself, acquired a sancity most profound.

These Five Thimbles were pearls of extraordinary size, fully three-quarters of an inch in length, and more than half an inch in breath. And in the end of each great pearl was a hollow running vertically. The pearls might have been placed on the fingers of a child, but they could not have been fitted over the digits of a grown person.

Nevertheless, that was no drawback to the belief that Buddha had worn them. In his case they would, of themselves, expand to the necessary diameter! It was exactly the same sort of belief as we of the West have in certain miracles, and may or may not have been true.

At any rate, these Five Pearl Thimbles became the ultimate sacred symbol of Buddhism, and for many centuries they lay in the ark, or coffer, of Buddha, in the inmost holy of holies in the Temple of Eternal Purity, in Canton. It can thus be understood that an upheaval was caused when they were stolen, and why the priesthood of the temple lost no time in setting out to track down the thief.

There are many unspeakable methods of tortures which have been evolved by the Chinese; terrible visitations which cannot be comprehended by us. Some of them rank as sheer devil work from a nether world, and it was the worst of these obscene tortures which had been visited upon the poor wretch who had stolen the pearls.

Sexton Blake was entirely out of sympathy with that. Blake did not deny that the priests had a perfect right to capture and punish the person who had defiled the holy of holies of the temple. It was desecration in its worst form, for no matter what the faith of a man or nation may be, that faith is entitled to respect.

But Blake drew the line at the means employed. And he did not mince matters with his old friend, Hong-Lo-Soo.

The latter, to give him his due, had lived long enough in the West to agree with Blake's point of view. What he may have thought the wretch deserved, and what he might have sanctioned in China, were different things.

He would have been content that the man should have been forced to disgorge and stand his punishment in a Western court. Moreover, the priests, true fanatics, had acted precipitately. They had destroyed the mind and soul of the thief, but they had recovered only one of the pearls; and their victim could never be made now to tell what had become of the others! It had developed into a pretty problem.

All this led up to the strange coincidence attendant upon the double murder at the house near Arundel, and the finding of the body of an unknown man in the Thames. That coincidence —the dead-white patch on the neck of each—was, Blake became convinced after his talk with Hong-Lo-Soo, nothing less than the terrible mark known among the Chinese as "wei-len-pung."

But why was that mark on the skin of these three dead Europeans? The victim of the priests' anger had been turned loose in the Bois, in Paris, with the same mark upon him. It was the stamp which showed to all men that the priestly orders had taken vengeance in its worst form. But what had the priests of Buddha to do with the man who had been shot dead while sitting at his desk in the house on the creek, near Arundel?

Why was it borne by the servant who had been found huddled at the bottom of the secondary staircase in the same house with a broken neck? And with the poor creature who had been fished out of the Thames the same night the other two had met their death?

The whole thing was so confusing from any point that it was most difficult to decide on a starting-point. Was the white mark borne by the three dead Europeans really the brand of "wei-len-pung"? If so, did it mean that the vengeance of the priests had been visited upon them? If so, was it on account of the Five Pearl Thimbles of Chen-tse? In that case, Blake could only conclude that the three dead Europeans must have had some connection in life with the great theft.

What linking up could there be between the unknown who was found floating in the river, and the original thief, Fu Won Chang? Between him and the man known as John Dean? Or the latter's servant, who, Blake had since learned, was known as Caleb Peters? And between the two latter and Fu Won Chang?

There was no denying the fact that it certainly looked as if John Dean had been in some profound state of fear on the night he met his death. There was the incident of all the lights in the house being on at an hour when the place was usually in darkness.

And who was Henry Dean, the so-called cousin, from Australia? That individual was still residing in the house on the creek. He was at perfect liberty to move about as he wished, but, nevertheless, the police were keeping an eye on him.

And again there was the woman in the case—the exotic creature who had taken Paris by storm some time before, and whom both

Blake and Tinker had seen in action, so to say. Blake did not attempt to deny that she was a most fascinating person, and he could understand well enough how a badly balanced individual like Fo Won Chang could lose his senses over her.

But so far as was known, she did not inspire the theft of the pearls. Hong-Lo-Soo's information — which could be depended on— was that Fu Won Chang had never been in Europe until he fled there after the theft. Therefore it did not seem that he could have had any acquaintance with the Bird of' Paradise before coming to Paris.

Not even Hong-Lo-Soo, in all his wisdom, and with all the information he could command, guessed for a single moment that Vali Mata-Vali had at one time been one of the girls of the temple from which the pearls had been stolen. Not that this had made her known to Fu Won Chang. That poor wretch had been as ignorant of her identity as Hong-Lo-Soo.

But the thing that weighed with Sexton Blake was the fact that it was she who had inspired such a passion in the breast of Fu Won Chang, that he had offered her nothing less than the sacred Five Pearl Thimbles of Chen-tse. Had she received any of the pearls from him before he was seized by the priests? Was the one they found on him the remaining gem of the lot which had already passed into her possession?

Detective-Inspector Thomas had taken personal charge of the affair at the house on the creek near Arundel. When he had left Hong-Lo-Soo that night, Blake had had a long talk with Thomas, telling him some, but not all, of what he had learned during the day. He spoke of the marks as being, in his opinion, a connecting link, and hinted that he had taken up a case that might touch on the murders.

In view of everything, Blake thought the man who had been fished out of the Thames might have been deliberately thrown in, and he suggested that Thomas should have every possible record examined in order to try and identify the fellow. Leaving the English end of it thus in Thomas' hands, he had determined to go to Paris and pick up, if possible, the loose ends of any threads which might be trailing adrift there.

Hence it was that he and Tinker were seated in front of the little cafe in the shadow of Notre Dame, at eleven o'clock in the morning, waiting for Inspector Journet, of the Surete, to appear. The French detective had been at work all the morning making certain inquiries for Blake, and it was only a few minutes past the hour when he came hurrying across the square in front of the cathedral.

"I think," he said briskly, when he had greeted them, "it would be better if we talked in a more private place." Blake rose at once.

"We can go along to the Carlitz, where I have a private sitting-room, if that is agreeable to you."

"Perfectly, Monsieur Blake."

They drove round in a taxi to the hotel in the Rue de Rivoli, and a few minutes later were seated in Blake's sitting-room. Inspector Journet drew out a blue-bound dossier and laid it on the table. Opening it, he scanned some of the papers inside; then he looked across the table at Blake.

"I think I have the information you wish, Monsieur Blake. This is the dossier of the woman in whom you are interested—Vali Mata-Vali. I shall leave it with you to examine fully at your leisure, but it will serve now if I give you the essentials."

"Thank you!"

"This woman arrived in France five years ago. Her dossier shows that she arrived from the East, and the details of the carte d'identite issued to her were taken from her answers to the usual formal questions and, of course, her passport. That document was issued in Saligon, and states that the woman in question is a French subject, born in Haiphong, French Indo-China; of age, twenty-one at the time the passport was issued, so she would now be about twenty-six. We have no reason to doubt the statements supplied by the passport, but, of course, you understand there is no guarantee that they are correct."

"A moment, please, Monsieur Journet. Would you say that she was pure French? The name does not sound like a French name."

"Nor is it. I do not know if she is pure French, but that is a difficult point to answer. You see, like your country, monsieur, we have many races, mixed and otherwise, under our care. In French Indo-China there are many people who would have other blood in them and yet call themselves French."

"I understand that. This name— Vali Mata-Vali—sounds as if it might, be Javanese."

"That is possible. Many Javanese have drifted up to that part of the China coast. I shall proceed. On her arrival in Paris she joined the chorus at the Folies Bergere, and for some time she seems to have been an unimportant member of the cast there. Then some two years or so ago she was brought out as a principal by Monsieur Gilbert of the Folies, who, I can only think, must have detected ability in her. At any rate, she took Paris by storm. She has danced, I believe, in London, but I do not know if she was popular there. It may be that, like the late Regine Flory, what appealed to a Paris audience did not win applause in London. She jumped into the very first rank in musical comedy here, and the salary paid her was very large. In a year she was a wealthy woman, and when she was well established she took a large house in a private park at St. Cloud. She is still resident in that house."

"So much for that phase of the matter. Now then, Monsieur Blake, not many weeks ago Vali Mata-Vali threw up her contracts. Her plea was, I am given to understand, a nervous breakdown. You have mentioned the affair of the Chinois who was found mentally deranged wandering about the Bois de Boulogne. You have also suggested that he paid considerable attention to Vali Mata-Vali. That is quite correct. It was on a night when he was going to see the woman that he disappeared, and, by a comparison of dates, I find that it was some two weeks after that he was found in the Bois. Where he was during that two weeks we cannot guess." (Blake had an idea, but said nothing.) "As no inquiries were made for this Chinois, nothing was known until he was found wandering. There are many suspicious circumstances about that affair which have not yet been cleared up. Vali Mata-Vali, however, made a statement to the police, but that did not help us any. Now you have asked about her recent movements. Your question has uncovered something of interest. A few weeks ago Vali Mata-Vali travelled to Tangier, Morocco. We have been in telegraphic touch with Tangier, and our information is that from Tangier she went south, by private caravan in the direction of Fez. It is not known exactly where she did go, and the curious thing is that the officials in Tangier have no record of how or when she left Morocco. Yet she is back in Paris—has been in residence at her house in St. Cloud for about ten days.

"That, monsieur, is a rough resume of what you will find in this dossier. I may add that we are not a little curious at the Surete to know why you wish these particulars. We have no desire to force your confidence, but if there is anything we can do to aid you we shall be happy to put ourselves at your disposal. I have had a talk with M. Dupuis, the Prefect, and he has instructed me to assure you that every facility you need will be at your service."

"Thank you, Monsieur Journet. Indeed, I am most grateful for what you have done. I am interested in this woman through a private case I have taken up, but it is not unlikely that I shall accept your offer and ask for your assistance. First, however, I wish to prosecute a few inquiries alone. After that—"

"Very good, monsieur; when you will.

"Oh, one more point, M. Blake. I forgot to say that Vali Mata-Vali is again performing at the Folies; she started to appear again two nights ago."

"Ah, that is an item of considerable interest! Take a note, Tinker, that we shall want seats for the Folies to-night."

Monsieur Journet took his departure soon after, promising to lend any further assistance when Blake should request it. Scarcely was he gone than a page tapped at the door with a telegram. On tearing it open Blake saw that it was from Inspector Thomas, and ran as follows;

"Finger-print records taken of man at morgue coincide exactly with those at Scotland Yard of ex-convict Sam Danvers, released about two years ago, and since then out of knowledge of police. Have just had telephone message from Inspector Arundel, inspector saying Henry Dean disappeared immediately after inquest verdict of which was wilful murder in each case against person or persons unknown. Every police force notified to be on look-out for Dean. Leave your discretion to inform Paris police and furnish description. Keep me advised.—THOMAS."

He passed the paper across to Tinker, who read it quickly. When he had finished he looked up, frowning.

"Sam Danvers — that name is familiar, guv'nor. Didn't we catch him in our net at some time or other?"

"Quite right, we did! He was a second-rate crook who used to work for Flash Brady when Brady was running that series of jewel frauds in London. After we closed up Brady's game the gang split, as you will remember, and I heard something about Danvers having been seen in America. Then he returned to London, where the Yard nabbed him and sent him up for three years. He disappeared as soon as he was released, but there was an affair in Australia about a year ago that made me think of Danvers. It was the sort of thing he might have been mixed up in if he had someone to direct him. A very mediocre sort of criminal, he was, but a nasty customer when he was working under the direction of someone else. But don't you see the second connection between his death and that of John Dean?"

"I don't quite get you, guv'nor."

"Henry Dean—the man who, according to this telegram, has cleared out. Don't you recall his saying he came from Australia?"

"Struth! So he did! And he might have known Danvers."

"Exactly! But that is not all. We have no proof of any sort that John Dean had been in Canada, as Henry Dean said. He may have been in Australia, or alternatively, neither Danvers nor Henry Dean may have been there. My idea that Danvers was one of the criminals mixed up in the affair I spoke of may be all wrong. Nevertheless, there is something queer about that phase of it, and, above all, we have that mark of 'wei-len-pung.' "

"Will this telegram alter our plans, guv'nor?"

"Not for to-night. We shall go to the Folies and have a look at this woman Vali Mata-Vali. In the meantime, we shall have lunch, and this afternoon make a call at the institute where the mentally deranged Chinaman has been taken. I believe there is an awful lot of nonsense talked about the new psycho-analysis, but there is no doubt that in careful hands a lot of good can be done in the treatment of certain mental cases along those lines. At any rate, I am going to try a very mild form of suggestion on Fu Won Chang and see what happens."

"I didn't know you intended seeing him. How will you fix it up?"

"It is already arranged. I got a permit from the Surete in case I should want it."

As soon as lunch was over Blake made a call that puzzled Tinker considerably. This was at the world-famous jewellery establishment of M. Acier in the Rue de la Paix. It was a good half-hour that the detective left his assistant to cool his heels on the pavement and when he did finally emerge he was entirely uncommunicative as to the purpose of his visit.

From that street of luxury shops they took a taxi to a certain address on the left bank of the river, far up the Boulevard Raspail. They drew up before a great gloomy-looking mansion, and after a considerable wait before the forbidding doors were finally admitted to a small, bare courtyard.

68

The man who unlocked the door to them was in a drab sort of uniform, with a drab, surly manner to match, but when Blake drew out the official permit bearing the signature, of the Prefect of Police the fellow's attitude underwent an abrupt change; M. Dupuis was a gentleman whom it would be unwise to cross, as every "agent," gendarme and prefect employee had learned very soon after his coming into office.

The man could not hide his surprise, however, when he found it was the demented Chinaman who was to be visited. It was the first time any but Official interest had been shown in that poor wretch since he had been brought to the house of restraint some weeks before, and, in the opinion of everyone at the home, his detention there was but a matter of a short time until he could be sent back to his own country.

However, that definite order could not be gainsaid, and the two visitors were taken along to a bare waiting-room where they were offered the use of two stiff wooden chairs, while the doorkeeper went off to find someone in higher authority. When this person arrived he proved to be a short, very stout man typical of the French official.

If the subordinate had seen no particular meaning in the name which M. Dupuis had written on the permit, the other had recognised at once the name of the famous English criminologist. His manner was effusive and almost fawning. The whole place and staff were completely at M. Blake's orders. He was greatly honoured by the visit of the very distinguished M. Blake, and so on and so on.

When the outburst was over Blake informed him quietly that while he was deeply appreciative of his kindness he had it in mind to visit but one inmate of the establishment—the unfortunate "Chinois," who had been found wandering in a demented condition in the Bois.

The other's shrewd little eyes showed how curious he was to know why Blake should wish to interview a person who was utterly incapable of realising his surroundings, much less make a coherent answer to any question. But Blake gave him not the slightest hint. Nor did he accept the superintendent's offer to enter and remain with him while he was in the room with the lunatic.

"I prefer that he should see no one connected with the Institute while I am with him," he said suavely. "I particularly impressed this upon my very dear friend, M. Dupuis."

The man could not go against that. If Blake was a "very dear friend" of the prefect, then it stood to reason that he would make a full report to the latter of his visit. So after a few words of warning as to the condition in which he would find the Chinaman, Blake and Tinker were conducted along to a small lift.

Entering this, they ascended to the second floor, where they were joined by a keeper. This individual was given explicit instructions from his chief, after which the whole party moved along another bare corridor until they came to a heavy wooden door near the end. While the keeper unlocked it Blake noticed there was a little wooden wicket set in the panel, and as he did not wish to be observed by curious eyes while he tried his experiment he drew the superintendent's attention to it.

"I intend putting into effect a certain test," he said easily, "one that may or may not prove successful. It is one in which M. Dupuis is deeply interested, and any small outside cause might tend to throw the subject off my influence. Will you be so good as to instruct this good fellow that he is not to peer through the wicket until I call him?"

Blake had asked that the order be given to the keeper, but it was a left-handed hint to anyone else of such a nature that the chief official himself could hardly ignore it. He assured Blake that he and his friend would be left entirely undisturbed until he should call, and at that the keeper opened the door.

The place to which Blake and Tinker had come was a sort of semi-state, semimunicipal asylum which, like all hybrid institutions, had to suffer on account of the haphazard attention of two sets of officials. It was of a kind that disappeared long ago in England, and, having been at some time or other hastily transformed from a private mansion to this purpose, there was a good deal lacking in what is nowadays considered even essential equipment.

The room into which they were ushered was a large, bare apartment, cold and gloomy to sight and feel. It had two curtainless windows, heavily barred, which looked out into a narrow light-well, and opposite were more barred windows for the gloomy contemplation of any inmate. For furniture there was a narrow iron bed on which was an old-fashioned sleeping pallet and one hard pillow.

There was nothing in the nature of a rug or carpet on the floor, and only a single hard, wooden chair for the unfortunate wretch who was interned, there to occupy. An iron washstand with a few toilet appurtenances was in a corner, and that was literally all. A more ghastly retreat for the mentally afflicted it would have been difficult to conceive.

Neither Blake nor Tinker could scarce repress a shudder as he viewed it. But the superintendent and the keeper appeared to consider it as quite fit for its purpose. To those men who regarded the mentally afflicted as an evil that should be eliminated, as one would dispose of a mad dog, it was far too good.

Such a thing as ministering to such wretches from the standpoint of a mental physician was utterly beyond their ken. All forms of aberration were to them crime. They could not understand how it could be regarded and treated as a disease.

The door closed after them, leaving them standing just on the inner side of the threshold peering through the half-gloom towards the far corner on the right, where the bed stood. They could see the rough outlines of a figure, which did not move even when Blake led the way towards the cot. Nor was it until he was close to the edge, peering down, that he saw it was indeed the mentally deranged Chinois.

It came as an acute shock to him to find himself gazing into deep, sloe-coloured eyes that were wide open and empty of expression as the painted china orbs of a doll. Not the faintest flicker of intelligence could he discern. They were just circles of flat colour. It was uncanny to know that there was physical and nervous life behind them —a life of which the connecting cord had been snapped.

The poor creature was wearing the same rags which had been about his thin, wasted body when he was found —ribboned shreds of once fine garments. His hair was pasty and unkempt, his face wrinkled like that of an old man, his thin-lipped mouth open and slack, showing the absence of control in even the lower facial muscles. He was an animate bundle of bone and flesh, a thing in which blood trickled in a sluggish circuit, that was all. Of mind-life he revealed no more than would have been found in a sawdust gollywog.

Sexton Blake's eyes were strangely pitiful and sympathetic as he studied the wreck that lay before him. At this close study the case seemed even worse than Hong-Lo-Soo had painted it. Until then Blake had been carrying with him a faint hope that he might hit on something that would fan some remaining spark of intelligence—a spark that he might watch glow into a flame that would consume the evil and obscene fetters that had driven the soul from its temple—

obscene because only such an influence could have done such terrible work.

And then he saw something.

Beneath the soiled red coverlet that had been thrown over the lower part of the body his gaze detected a slight movement. It was just a steady movement of the cloth at a certain spot, and ever so gently. Blake turned down the rug. Then both he and Tinker could see that the movement was an actual muscular functioning of the right hand of the patient—a slow, steady rubbing of the tips of the fingers against the palm.

In a European that would have indicated little or nothing beyond visible movement which must have its origin from some faint, very faint glimmer away back in the brain. But in the case of a Chinaman of the mandarin caste it meant a good deal to Blake, for it was almost positive proof that not only was the message coming down the arm from an almost dormant part of the brain, but that somewhere back in the deeps of that seat of life was definite association of some habit with the brain-message.

What could that habit be? In a Celestial what did it indicate? It suggested to Blake that, like so many of his fellow countrymen the poor wretch before him—this emaciated wreck who had once been Prince Fu Won Chang —had been accustomed to soothe his mind by rolling two polished walnuts against each other in one hand.

It was a thing he had done himself when in China disguised as one of the race, and on more than one occasion he had found the habit growing on him, had felt the same soothing which it brought to those who indulged in it.

He shot a meaning look at Tinker, and then made a gesture to him. Between them they pulled the bed round so that the miserable light that came in at the window fell full upon the deeply lined features. Then Blake seated himself upon the side of the cot, and took something from his pocket.

He held up a round, whitish object for Tinker to see, and as his assistant's gaze took in the smooth, creamy surface of what appeared to be a gigantic pearl, he almost gasped in amazement. His expression grew more puzzled than ever when Blake drew out a second sphere that was seemingly an exact duplicate of the first. And then suddenly Tinker realised why Blake had visited the jewellery establishment in the Rue de la Paix.

He watched while Blake gently insinuated both spheres under the moving finger-tips of the sick man's hand, and then they both bent over breathless to watch what the effect would be.

CHAPTER 9.   The Light of Intelligence.

AT first it seemed as if the man on the bed was quite unaware that something solid had come under the frictioning fingers. The same mechanical motion was kept up, round and round and round, but one thing Blake did notice—the two spheres were rolled and rubbed smoothly and kept perfectly in position as only could have been done by one long accustomed to the habit. Was there any additional flicker of intelligence there, or was it a purely automatic response of the nervous centres?

Blake rose now, and, walking round the bed, sat down on the other side so the light fell full on his own features as well. Then, with a motion to Tinker to stand by in case of need, he put one arm under the patient's shoulders. The latter made no attempt at resistance when Blake lifted him into a sitting position—was as unconsciously compliant as a sack of feathers would have been.

Still Blake persisted in his efforts. He worked his hand up until it was placed behind the other's ear, and then very gently he twisted the head round so the eyes were in a direct line with his own. Holding the other thus, he put out his free hand and caught hold of that in which the spheres were being rolled.

The pressure he exerted was so gradual that it was scarcely perceptible, and when his own strong, brown hand had closed over the thin, bony, yellow one, he drew it up so that it was just between them. Now he gave a jerk of his head to Tinker.

"Get round on the other side and steady his back," he whispered.

When Tinker had obeyed, Blake could free his right arm in order to bring it round and use it with his left. Prising open the Chinaman's fingers he took out the two spheres, gently restraining the mechanical movements of the muscles so that any flicker of intelligence there might be in the mind would be disturbed in that one form of functioning, which seemed to be the only link it held with the past sensate life of the poor wretch.

Still holding the hand with his left, he opened the right, allowing the two creamy spheres to roll into his palm, canting his hand a little so the objects must come within the line of the other's vision. Then, in a low, monotonous, vibrant tone he began to speak, using just a few simple words in Chinese.

"Look at me, Fu Won Chang—look at me—think of the Five

Pearl Thimbles of Chen-tse—look at me, Fu Won Chang—look, at me with the eyes of intelligence—look through the light of the moon-washed stream of the Five Classics—come from the valley into the brilliant flame given forth by the Son of the Heavens—look at the brilliancy of the Five Great Pearls of Chen-tse— see the effulgence of the sacred Thimbles of the Buddha—look at me. Fu Won Chang—look—listen to the voice from the place of light—the shadow of Chen-tse is no more—the refulgent glory of the Five Pearl Thimbles is before you—look at them, Fu Won Chang—your honourable ancestors are seeking you—"

On and on the voice kept up its monotonous chant, sometimes repeating phrases already used or inventing new ones which bore on the same subject, yet always insisting on the regions of mental and spiritual fight. What Blake was attempting was nothing more than a simple scientific method of breaking down the hypnotic wall that had been erected about Fu Won Chang's mind. Even when he had been talking with Hong-Lo-Soo he had come to the conclusion that it was some form of so-called permanent hypnotism that had been visited upon the poor wretch.

In some cases there was no means of bringing back intelligence to a mind so bedamned; not even those who had perpetrated the outrage could undo their work without a proper subject to work on. Blake knew perfectly well that among the adepts of India and the Far East, there exists a form of hypnotism which is almost unknown to us of the West, and certainly its practice is far, far from the simple forms of mind control which are seen exhibited on the variety stage.

But he had made a deep study of the science, and now he was using every atom of his will-power to dominate and drive out the suggestions of the priests who had sent Fu Won Chang out into the world when they had finished with him—a mindless and soulless being.

For a good half-hour or more he talked to the shrivelled creature he was holding before him. Not for a moment did he remove his eyes from the flat orbs that he forced to keep on a level with his. And, constantly, he kept up a slight movement of the two spheres in his hand, so that they should be an attraction within the focus of the other's gaze.

It was one of the strangest dramas in which he and Tinker had ever taken part, and one of the saddest. No matter of what race or creed or colour a man may be, there is something monstrous and awful in finding him but a breathing, insensate thing, without a single visible sign of the divine spark.

There was a devil of horror within that human temple, and Sexton Blake was determined to drive it out if his will could reach it.

And yet it was Tinker who sensed the first change. Holding Fu Won Chang at the back as he was, one hand lay against the spinal cord, and it was here, close to where the main nervous cable lay, that he felt a slight quivering. He leant forward, whispering:

"I've felt something, guv'nor—a sort of quiver close to the spine."

Blake nodded without removing his gaze from Fu Won Chang's eyes. But the sudden beads of sweat that started out on his forehead revealed how the words had broken in upon his intense concentration of mind and will. His lips moved ever so slightly.

"Stroke the spine gently with your finger tips," Tinker heard him say; and he obeyed.

Now, if it were possible, Blake increased the bombardment of his will upon the blank screen of the Celestial's mind. His eyes had narrowed to glittering points of blue ice; every nerve within him was tuned to concert pitch; every faculty of that fine brain was striving, striving to get the low tuning of the other's mind.

Fully another half-hour went by, and had it not been for the fear of M. Dupuis' anger, it is almost certain that someone would have tapped at the door by now. Had such an interruption come it would have ruined everything that had gone—would have roused in Sexton Blake an anger such as he had rarely been seen to exhibit. For Blake was beginning to feel the insidious twinge of exhaustion trying to undermine the terrific pressure under which his mind was functioning.

But it did not come, and he knew from the way Tinker was moving his head that he had felt that faint quivering along the spinal column. Still Blake persisted, watching for the first hint that the nerve uneasiness which Tinker had sensed was reaching the eyes, which are in truth the windows of the soul.

And then a fresh beading of water burst from the pores of his skin as a faint flicker of light showed in those flat, brown orbs. Or was it a flicker? he asked himself. It seemed to have shown like some tiny spark in the deeps, then it was gone.

He was breathing as if he had been running a great distance. His eyes had narrowed more than ever, and never before had Tinker seen them such an icy blue as now. Blake's jaws were clenched until a hard lump stood out close to each lobe of the ears; his lips were a hard, straight line from which every shred of blood had been pressed. The whole face had gone taut; the skin seemed stretched across it as if the angle of the bones must burst through.

And then it came again.

That spark. Oh, so faint it was, flickering just in the centre of the brown orbs, giving them life, giving them soul.

And it stayed.

There came a sudden stiffening of the neck muscles. Fu Won Chang seemed unaware of Blake and Tinker. His head bent a little while his eyes fixed themselves on the two creamy spheres which rolled gently back and forth in the hollow of Blake's hand. His head advanced, his lids moved, and his breath sounded audibly.

Still Blake kept up his chant, voicing the supreme power of light and the nothingness of shadow; uttering the name of Buddha and of Chen-tse; harping again and again on the honourable ancestors of Fu Won Chang; playing on every chord which must lay in the deepest part of the nature of every Celestial.

And still that spark of soul stayed.

Slowly, Blake drew his right hand back. Fu Won Chang thrust his head after it as if it drew him like a magnet. Then his own hand came up, and a tentative finger went out towards the two spheres. Blake held his hand steady, and waited while that adventuring finger crossed the tips of his own digits and continued on until it hovered just over his palm. Down came the finger until at last it touched one of the spheres.

That contact was like the shock of a thousand volts to the nervous system of Fu Won Chang. The crisis that Sexton Blake had known must be risked came with an explosion. The Chinaman stiffened like a board, every muscle and tendon rigid as steel. Then from his throat came a gasping cry, followed by a high-pitched scream that made Tinker's blood run cold.

Followed the convulsions.

It took every atom of the joint physical strength possessed by Blake and Tinker to force the demented creature back on to the bed. While that terrible upheaval held him it was only possible to keep him from running amok—to wait for the result. When the convulsions were past he might be worse than before, if such a thing were possible; or, faint hope, the devil of horror that lay within him might pass with the constriction.

The door opened, and the amazed keeper looked in. Blake was oblivious to the intrusion, for his back was towards the door. But Tinker saw the man, and waved him away. The keeper hesitated, but finally decided to obey until he could find his chief.

Then once more the two were left to fight the last phase of the battle, and, as the convulsions began to grow less, as the frantic twistings began to wear themselves out and the screams died away to whimperings and moanings, Blake managed to get out a flask of brandy he had brought with him. While he held it with one hand, Tinker reached over and unscrewed the cap.

Blake forced a generous dose between Fu Won Chang's lips, and held his head up so that he must swallow the raw spirit. Then he set the flask aside and continued to watch.

By this time the superintendent was at the door. He entered in a rush, waving his arms, and demanding to know what torture was being visited upon his patient. Blake's nerves were at the ragged edge, and he did not choose his words.

"Get out!" he snarled. "Get out quick! By Heaven, I'll see that M. Dupuis hears of this. Get out!"

And the awed, and now frightened, man "got."

Blake turned back to Fu Won Chang, and once more began to speak to him in simple Cantonese. He moved the other's head so he could see his eyes, and then a great throb went through him as he saw Fu Won Chang gazing up at him with a steady light of intelligence showing in his sloe-black orbs.

They had won. The black devil of horror had been driven out to stay. Fu Won Chang had been brought back to the places of light. From somewhere in the great deeps of the cosmos, his soul had come hurrying back, once more to assume dominion over its appointed temple.

And then, for perhaps the first time in his life, Sexton Blake fainted clean away. It was the price he paid of his own will and mind and strength of spirit to give sanity back to that haggard, yellow wreck that lay before him.

CHAPTER 10. George Marsden Plummer Visits the Chinese Priests—and Sam Danvers Falls Into His Clutches.

THE more Plummer learned of his new partner, the more he was forced to admire her acuteness of mind and reckless daring. They were of a calibre he had never before come across in any woman of European race, and, while realising that she may or may not have told him the truth about her parentage, he was inclined to think that there was a fairly substantial streak of the subtle Oriental in her nature.

It might be explained by the influence of the environment of shadowy intrigue of the temple in her young and most impressionable years; but that didn't matter two straws to him. All that counted was the fact that she measured up one hundred per cent in every way, not omitting her extraordinary physical charm.

What had been at the back of her mind when she was philandering with Fu Won Chang he didn't know, and didn't bother to try to find out. He doubted very much if she herself could have told him. But it was plain that either consciously or unconsciously she had dragged from the Manchu all the information she could regarding the five great pearls which were their present objective.

She was able to place at Plummer's disposal certain items of information which were to prove invaluable. To Vali Mata-Vali, the names of those who had been accomplices of Fu Won Chang after the theft meant nothing; to Plummer one, at least, gave a clue which he was not slow to make use of.

This name—Sam Danvers—suggested as much to Plummer as it was to mean to Sexton Blake, when it was to reach him through Inspector Thomas, of Scotland Yard. Plummer had by no means lost touch with the underworld of London since his sojourn in Morocco, and through his numerous correspondents he had kept pretty well au fait with most of the major events that had taken place.

As a matter of fact, at the time of the series of jewel frauds which had been carried out some years before, he had had a personal interest in the doings of Flash Brady. He had known when Sam Danvers had been "sent up," and he had heard later when the crook had been released.

After that he had lost sight of him, but when, through certain somewhat fragmentary notes which Vali supplied, he came upon a similar name, his mind at once jumped to the Sam Danvers he had known. It was on that one bit of information that Plummer planned his campaign, a good deal of material in Paris, and when he had sorted this out, Plummer resolved on a bold stroke.

This was nothing less than to enter the lair where the Chinese priests of the Temple of Eternal Purity lay in hiding, and face them with what he knew, trusting in his own capacity for bluff to make his own terms. It was obvious that to work at cross-purposes with these yellow hounds would be to add unnecessary risk to the whole game. If he found them where he hoped to find them, then it would be plain that they had reached a blind end.

Plummer had certain avenues of information of his own in Paris, and he had lost no time in discovering just what had become of Fu Won Chang after the fiends from Canton had finished with him and turned him adrift.

The great point on which his plans turned was this: Had the priests secured only one of the pearls from Fu Won Chang, as Vali Mata-Vali thought? Or had they secured the lot? If the latter were the case, then there was little likelihood of his finding them still in Paris. They would lose no time in getting back to their own country, and within the safe walls of the Temple of Eternal Purity. On the other hand, if they had only torn one gem from Fu Won Chang, then it was plain that for once the cunning Oriental had overreached himself—using the noun in a collective sense.

In this case, what would they be doing now? Had they reached an impasse? If they had, then they might be more than willing to listen to whatever proposals he—Plummer—might have to make. Plummer wanted those five pearls for only one reason—for the actual money they would bring to him and Vali Mata-Vali. He realised, and she agreed, that it would be far too risky for her to keep them as ornaments to wear.

Besides, their partnership was one in which neither of them would be led astray by any sentimental nonsense of that sort. It was riches they were after, and nothing else. Unless, of course, the fear of the past could be removed from her present, and if he could get the whip hand of the priests, Plummer had little doubt he would be able to secure that.

Hence it was that a week or so before Sexton Blake travelled down into Sussex with Inspector Thomas to investigate the puzzling double murder that had taken place in the house on the creek near

Arundel, George Marsden Plummer left the historic, old chateau which Vali Mata-Vali had purchased at St. Cloud, and while she was going through her act at the Folies Bergere, he was making his way along a small street in the Montparnasse quarter, on the left bank of the Seine— that district where so many foreigners find a refuge in Paris.

It should be mentioned here, perhaps, that it had been decided wise, for the present, at least, that Vali Mata-Vali should resume her appearance at the Folies, as if she had nothing of a more serious nature on her mind. Also, the forked beard which Plummer had affected in Morocco, had now disappeared, leaving his chin as smooth as it had been in his early days of crime. It had the additional asset of making disguise easier.

Plummer was quite certain of his destination. His information had come from a source that could be depended on. Therefore, when he had turned into a short, narrow cul-de-sac, it only by a single standard-lamp at the entrance, he did not waste time examining door after door.

The whole place was a warren with which he had been well acquainted in days gone by; the particular corner of that warren where the priests of the Temple of Eternal Purity lived, and had their being in a state of miserable nostalgia, was a small box of an apartment on the third floor in the lower left-hand corner of the cul-de-sac.

Reaching the door, he pushed it open and pressed the catch of a pocket flash-lamp. Directly in front of him was a flight of rickety stairs, which he started to climb with no attempt to hide the sound of his movements. A good many queer folk entered and left those warrens in the night hours, and the passage of one could evoke no comment.

From the first floor he continued his progress to the second, and so on to the third. Arriving there, he could see no signs of a light showing through any chink, even though he flashed off his torch for a few moments. But just ahead of him was a door, and, when he again switched on the light and had taken out a small automatic pistol, he lifted one foot and drove the door inwards with a crash.

A startled chorus of sharp exclamations greeted this unceremonious action. Plummer had a swift vision of three Celestials seated on mats, with a single candle and bowl of rice in the centre of the circle, when he was over the threshold, kicking the door closed as he stood inside. Then he grinned evilly at the amazed priests whom he was keeping covered with the pistol. He had picked up a good deal of Cantonese during the years he had kicked about the China coast, and now he used it.

He had decided that his best plan was to bring things to a head immediately, and carry them through while the going was good. Besides, time was the essence of the matter, so far as he and Vali Mata-Vali were concerned.

"Hoo-la-ma," he grunted in a guttural imitation of the age-old Chinese greeting. "I trust I find your most honourable persons in the best of health and still enjoying the favour of the sublime and much-to-be-revered Buddha."

The eldest of the three (if any difference in age could be said to be apparent), a wrinkled, wizened old wretch, who might have been a hundred and forty, was calm enough now. Strangers did not burst in upon the sacred priests of the Temple of Eternal Purity with this lack of ceremony even if those priests were in Paris unless they knew what ground they were walking on. And that pistol settled matters. His hands slid into the loose sleeves of his tunic; and his old eyes were almost hidden in wary slits as he mumbled: "Ho-hang-ho, honoured sir. Our poor and wretched abode is not fit to entertain one of such honourable magnificence."

Plummer laughed. They could dissemble as they might, but he knew they were afire with uneasiness and curiosity to know who he was and what could be the purpose of his visit. He might, for all they knew, be a representative of the Paris Surete.

If he had had more time at his disposal it would have amused him to keep them on tenterhooks for some time longer, but he was there to finish the business as quickly as possible, and it suited him to give them a further shock.

"We shall dispense with formalities," he said abruptly. "I have come to talk of the Five Pearl Thimbles of Chen-tse."

He could not have created more sensation if he had dropped a bomb among them. They did not leap or yell, but, in so far as their natures would permit them to show their feelings outwardly, they did so in a united and long-drawn

"A-i-e!"

Again Plummer laughed.

"Yes, my honourable friends," he went on, "I have come to talk about the Five Sacred Thimbles of Buddha which were stolen from the secret treasure ark in the holy of holies of the Temple of Eternal Purity by the Gate of the Tiger in Canton. It will save time if you will realise that I know all about the matter and all about how you overplayed your hand in the case of Fu Won Chang. We shall talk now, if you please. If you refuse to heed what I say you will find that you will be sent out of this country to-morrow; and that would be a pity when you have only succeeded in regaining one of the sacred thimbles. I have come, my honourable friends, to tell you how you may secure the other four thimbles. Am I to be listened to?"

There was an almost imperceptible stirring of the three; then, in low, guttural accents, the eldest again spoke.

"Thy words are as pearls of wisdom, honourable one. Speak, for we heed."

Nor did they know, cunning adepts though they were, what an inward sigh of relief Plummer gave. Those words told him that Vali was right—they had overplayed their hand with Fu Won Chang, and they must have got possession of only one of the stolen gems. He knew now that he could run on a strong line.

And he did. He still took the precaution to keep the three covered with the pistol, and he invited them suavely to remove their hands empty from their sleeves. That done, he squatted on his heels and began to talk. For several minutes his voice droned on in broken Cantonese, which they understood well enough, and from time to time, when he paused a throaty question was asked. He was prompt with his answers. He had his proposals crystal clear. It was something to which they could answer a simple "Yes" or "No." And before an hour went by the answer was "Yes."

But that was by no means the end of the confab. Plummer was closeted with the three for a good two hours longer, and when he finally did emerge into the cul-de-sac he had gained more than he had gone after, for with him he took away an oddly fashioned little bamboo disc with a jade facing about the size of an English half-crown, and, in a tiny jade phial, a small supply of a colourless liquid, which, when applied in the quantity of a drop or so to the jade face of the disc and applied to the human skin caused a mark more pallid than death itself—the dread mark known as "wei-len-pung"—the vengeance mark of the priests of Buddha.

He returned to the chateau at St. Cloud to announce his success, and if he looked for any immediate reward, he had it in the sudden flame that came into the usually enigmatical eyes. There were depths in Vali Mata-Vali that Plummer was only beginning to plumb.

The next scene in his campaign was laid in London. Equipped as a conventional traveller in silks, he travelled across the Channel by aeroplane, taking two orthodox cases of samples with him. He took up his quarters in a certain small hotel on the fringe of the Soho district, and from that base started his search for Sam Danvers.

Plummer figured that Danvers would make for London if he found it necessary to lie low, for it was the haunts of the great metropolis that he knew better than any other. And Plummer, shrewd crook that he was, had figured dead right.

First here and then there he heard a whisper and a hint that brought him closer to his quarry every hour.

He had a dozen or more old associates working on his behalf, and many a strange message came to the hotel the wording of such a nature that only one who had been initiated into the jargon could have understood the meaning.

Then, one night he received an urgent summons that took him into the riverside purlieus of Wapping. He reached the place by river, and by way of some rickety steps gained an old wharf at the back of a building that was a hotbed of criminal plotting.

It was both jumping-off place and temporary hiding for those higher up in the fraternity, and in there, Plummer now knew, Sam Danvers lay concealed. Not only that, but Sam Danvers was paying his way in a fashion that meant money—plenty of it.

And so, at a moment when he was seated at a table reading an evening paper and getting through a bottle of whisky—indulging himself in the top degree of comfort, according to his ideas—Sam Danvers, ex-lag, found his eyes rising slowly and strange shivers running up and down his spine as a key turned in his door and the portal swung open slowly.

Sam Danvers clawed for his gun, but a steady hand that came round the edge of the door beat him to it. The hand was followed by a body, and then a startled curse broke from Danvers' throat as he recognised the hard features of that once notorious criminal, George Marsden Plummer.

Plummer meant business, and the lesser crook could see it. One word was enough to bring his hand back on to the table, and he sat quiet while Plummer closed the door and walked across towards him.

"Where is that pearl?" demanded Plummer harshly. "Get it out quick! Then I want some information out of you."

Danvers gulped.

"I don't know whatcher talking abaht!" he stammered. "Purl—I don't know nuthink abaht any purl!"

Plummer leant over the table without haste, and then the room resounded with the violent smack of hand upon flesh as he struck Danvers a violent blow across the side of the face.

"I said pearl," he repeated, without raising his voice. "Get it out!"

If Sam Danvers hadn't been soaking in whisky for a considerable time past some grains of sense might have remained to him. But at the smashing blow some fragments of courage rode up on the alcoholic surge that filled him, and he answered with a word that he would have considered it sheer madness to use in a more sober moment. It was almost the last word that Sam Danvers ever voiced.

George Marsden Plummer thrust his weapon back into his pocket. For several reasons he did not wish to use it there. Then he made one leap that carried him round the table, and, catching hold of Danvers, he jammed him back until man and chair crashed to the floor.

Holding his victim thus, Plummer wrapped one arm about his throat, closing it in more and more tightly until the pressure cut off every possibility of breathing. The other crook struggled frantically, but he might as well have beaten against a stone wall.

He was in the grip of one of the most deadly holds ever used by the Moors—one that it had taken Plummer many weeks to master; and from it there was no escape. It was a killing hold that left practically no marks—a useful trick to know when one was scouting through mountain passes at night, and equally valuable in the game the master-criminal was playing. It was the return of George Marsden Plummer with a vengeance.

When Plummer eased his hold, what had been Sam Danvers slid to the floor. Then Plummer went to work methodically. First he stripped the other to the skin and examined every stitch of his clothing. Wherever he found a maker's label or laundry mark he removed it, emptying every pocket as he went along. It was, however, from a small compartment in a belt that Danvers had been wearing about his waist that Plummer found what he had been seeking—one of the Five Pearl Thimbles of Chen-tse. For a few moments he permitted himself to gaze upon that wondrous jewel before placing it in his own pocket.

His next action was to take out the bamboo disc with the jade face which had been given to him by the priests of Chen-tse in Montparnasse. On that face he smeared a drop of the liquid which was in the small jade phial; then he pressed the circle of jade against the neck of the dead man.

Instantly there appeared on the skin a round mark as white as snow—the brand of "wei-len-pung." Who would ever connect that mark with George Marsden Plummer? And what cared the priests of Chen-tse if it were recognised as their brand?

After that he re-clothed his victim. This done, he turned out the light and opened the window. Half a minute later something went turning and tumbling through the air to fall into the water of the Thames a few feet beyond the end of the short jetty, something that was destined to be found a little over twenty-four hours later by the river police.

Plummer closed the window and carefully drew the blind. Feeling his way across the room he turned on the light and made his way to the table. In the chair that had been so recently occupied by Sam Danvers he sat while he made a close examination of the odds and ends he had taken from Danvers' pockets.

He discarded most of them as soon as he had given them a cursory glance; but now and then he laid an object aside. When he came to the end he began a re-scrutiny of these latter, mostly bits of dirty paper on which the late crook had scribbled words or notes.

One pile of Treasury notes and some silver Plummer carefully pocketed. Everything in the form of negotiable cash was always grist to Plummer's mill.

It was among the bits of paper that he found what he had been seeking. From these he composed a fairly legible sequence of items that told him as much as he needed to know; and as he completed his work he nodded his head several times in a satisfied way.

"I might have overplayed my hand, bumping him off so soon," he muttered. "That would have been as big a fool play as the priests made. But I had a hunch a bird like Danvers wouldn't trust to his memory, and that sort of a guy carries all he owns about with him. I guess this will about put the can on Mr. John Dean & Co. I'll tickle him up with a letter that will keep him guessing, and get it posted to-night so it will reach him before I arrive on the scene. If he gets wind of what has happened to Danvers he'll do a bolt before I can put the brand on him, and it's too risky for me to stay in England a moment longer than I have to. But if I give him a hint that someone is coming to see him about Fu Won Chang, someone whom he had better see, he won't know whether it is friend or foe.

"From some of this stuff here it is plain that Danvers knew what had happened to Fu Won Chang. That seems to have sent the whole bunch leery. Danvers had certainly lost his nerve. And I fancy I'll find Dean about as jumpy. Anyway, a letter can't do any harm and it is pretty certain to keep him in that house down in Sussex until I get there. He won't have time to figure out any plan of action after he gets that letter and he won't dare clear off and let the person who writes the letter turn up in his absence. I guess I've got the psychological bulge on this gang all right. But I'll say it was a slick piece of work all the same."

Just exactly what Plummer meant by the last words will become apparent later as this record unfolds.

So, when he had committed to memory all he needed to know of the somewhat scrappy story contained on those crumpled bits of paper which had formed the complete filing system of the unfortunate Sam Danvers, Plummer methodically gathered up every scrap he had taken from the other's pockets and burned them in the grate. Then after a careful look round the room he turned out the light and departed as he had come. He paused only once on his way to the street— he was leaving the place in the opposite direction to which he had come— to whisper to a man who stole out of a dark room; then he passed down the last flight of stairs and a few minutes later was striding with perfect sangfroid through the narrow streets of Wapping.

CHAPTER 11.   Plummer's Movements in England—And His Audacity in Face of His Crime.

ONLY a first-class set of brains with a considerable experience of human nature could have risked sending what could, in a way, be regarded as a warning to the person who was marked down as a victim, it was a thing which the ordinary crook would never have dreamed of doing. He would have feared that such uneasiness would be aroused that the recipient would decamp without loss of time.

But Plummer, a past master in the art of thinking just one jump ahead of the other man in the game, figured differently. From what he had learned through Vali Mata-Vali, and what he had made into a coherent sequence from the bits of paper taken from Sam Danvers' pockets, he knew that a certain person calling himself John Dean had played no little part in the affair of the Five Pearl Thimbles of Chen-tse.

The information he gained that night in Wapping told him more. It was sufficient for him to make a pretty good guess as to how Sam Danvers had happened to get drawn into a game that, normally, was away out of his class. These scraps that gave bits of clues which Plummer could read scraps such as a bit of old racing programme for Moonee Valley course outside Melbourne; a torn voucher of a ticket in the famous Australian Tattersalls' sweep; a pawn ticket made out by a Sydney pawnbroker; and, last but by no means least, the tabs on some of the outer garments bore the name of a Melbourne clothing merchant. Proof enough there that Sam Danvers had been in Australia fairly recently.

Now Plummer knew nothing of a certain affair in Australia that had taken place a year or so before, in which Sexton Blake had seen the work of the same Sam Danvers. But Plummer could read between the lines, so to say, and he was as certain that the John Dean, whose address he found among the bits of paper, was mixed up in the business which was of such interest to him just then as if Sam Danvers had told him.

Hence, considering the success that had attended his efforts this night in Wapping, he thought it a pretty good gamble to make his second step a journey to Sussex.

Therefore, in accordance with his avowed intention, he wrote a brief letter to John Dean at the address which he had found, and duly posted it that same night, it would catch the last collection possibly, but if it did not reach John Dean until the following afternoon Plummer would be just as well satisfied.

He was calculating that Dean would be in such a quandary; that he would not have time to make up his mind whether a friend or enemy was about to visit him—whether to sit tight or make a bolt. The writing of that letter was a bit of artistry that could have been understood and appreciated by a student of human nature such as Sexton Blake.

All the next day Plummer was busy making his arrangements. He knew that what he had to do in England must be done swiftly, and that every stroke must be aimed with surety. A single mis-step would be fatal. He would not be able to draw back and make a second attempt. He was too vivid a personality in the criminal world, and he was "wanted" too badly by Scotland Yard to take undue risks.

One whisper that he was in England, and not only Sexton Blake, his old enemy, but every man out of Scotland Yard would have a line out for him. Therefore his plans, while seemingly elaborate, were made with a careful eye to every eventuality. How they worked out will be seen.

One thing he soon found would be necessary was a trustworthy accomplice. The country round about Arundel was well known to Plummer, and by refreshing his memory with the aid of an ordnance map—one inch to the mile—he soon had a clear mental picture of the immediate area of country surrounding the house on the creek, which was his objective.

This certainty of knowledge was as important as the accomplice, and the latter was not difficult to find in the underworld of London. During the afternoon he paid his bill at the hotel where he had been staying, and from that moment Monsieur Stein, traveller in French silks, disappeared entirely from the ken of those with whom he had had any association during the past day or two.

His first care was to pay a visit to a certain little shop in Whitechapel, where for a very substantial fee one could have one's face treated with wax injections with as much efficiency as could have been obtained at the shop of the most fashionable dermatologist in Regent Street—and no questions asked.

When he finally emerged from that place he was a radically different looking person from the man who had gone in, and from that moment, too, his name became a new one. Henry Dean he chose to call himself for the time being, but since he did not expect to have to use the same cognomen to anyone but, possibly, the other crook who had adopted the same surname, it didn't matter much.

By dusk he was seated in a certain rendezvous with his accomplice, instructing him at length just what he had to do that night, and then, since he had anticipated every possible contingency, Plummer sought a back room and lay down.

Shortly after midnight a small two-seater car, painted the ubiquitous grey, travelled unostentatiously out of London and along the Portsmouth road. At Guildford it swung off on to the Horsham road, and after passing through that sleeping town, turned towards Petworth and Pulborough. From Petworth it drove slowly until a spot was reached in the very middle of some heavy beech woods that line the road just to the north of the little village of Bury. And there the car came to a stop.

From it there stepped a tall man, who stood upright, listening. A dog howling in the distance was the only sound that broke the stillness, so he thrust his head and shoulders back under the hood, emerging presently with a small bundle tied with string.

He laid this on the running-board and removed the overcoat he had been wearing. In giving this to the man who sat at the wheel he received in return a longish object, bladed at each end, which looked like a small, light double paddle; and indeed, that is exactly what it was. With this under one arm and the package he had laid on the running-board under the other, he paused long enough to whisper:

"Wait, as I said, about three-quarters of an hour, and then drive on slowly to the spot I marked. You can't miss that side road, and don't forget—dowse your lights. If a policeman does come along, get busy on your engine. I shall be along as soon as I finish, and I don't expect the job will take long once I get into the house."

With that he turned, and a moment or so later his figure was lost in the gloom of the beeches.

Plummer picked his way carefully. He knew that somewhere near the spot where he had entered the woods he should pick up a path, but he thought it too risky to switch on his flash-lamp until he was well away from the road.

There was nothing very unusual in the lights of a stationary motor-car, out if any local constable should see a flare swinging through the woods, he would at once become curious. And Plummer considered it of the utmost importance that his visit to the house on the creek should be "wrapt in mystery."

Luck was with him, for he had descended a sloping bit scarcely a score of yards when he knew by the feel of the ground beneath his feet that he was on a path. Now he risked the light for a few seconds, and as he saw a well-defined track winding down before him he grunted in a satisfied way.

Further on, as he proceeded, he brought the flash-lamp into use once more, but mostly he trusted to his own senses, and he knew, some minutes later, that he was right, for just beneath him lay the black surface of water reflecting the stars, it was the little river Arun, that winds along through that part of Sussex to empty its waters into the sea at Littlehampton.

Plummer knew that the Arun is a tidal river, and that afternoon he had ascertained that it would be high water in the vicinity of Bury about three o clock in the morning. He would have found it better for his purpose had the tide reached its zenith an hour earlier, for that would have meant he could have utilised it during the whole campaign he had planned for the night.

But it was better that he should have the flow against him now than later when speed might mean all the difference between discovery or not; and at any rate, it was so near the top of the flood now that the inflow was lessening.

He paused on the bank of the river and laid the double-bladed paddle on the ground. It took but a few moments to remove the cord from the package, and when that was done he proceeded to unroll what would have appeared to be, in better light, several flat folds of rubber. when these were completely released he leant over the object, which was now hanging about his nether limbs like a rubber blanket, and taking the mouth of a valve between his lips, began to blow.

Again and again and again he filled his lungs for the effort, and slowly, as he kept up the blowing, the rubber sides of the object began to fill, growing larger and rounder until they appeared as a gigantic rubber sausage rectangular in shape, with jointed corners and a strong rubber panelled bottom. When he had finished he had before him just one of those folding rubber boats which have become so popular for river paddling during the summer months.

It wasn't much of a craft as such go, but it was capable of

carrying two full-grown persons, was remarkably light, and easy to negotiate, and when finished with, could be deflated and carried away just as easily as he had brought it along.

He slid it over the bank until it was floating light as a cork on the surface. Then very gingerly he got in, resting first on one knee, then on the other. When it was quite steady he sank back so that his legs were out straight in front of him, and then, grasping up the paddle from the bank close to him, he pushed off.

As has been said, the tide was still running in, but in that light rubber coracle it was not difficult paddling, and, in any event, Plummer was not anxious to make great speed. His chief concern was to slip past Bury and under the bridge at Houghton without attracting any attention.

He was quite aware that along the stretch of water both above and below the Houghton bridge he might find houseboats moored, and these would be a certain danger, particularly if anyone was sleeping on deck. But that was a gauntlet that had to be run.

He stole past Bury without seeing a soul, keeping in close to the bank until he could see the pointed stone tower of the little church silhouetted against the starlit sky. Then he expended more effort, until he saw something white on the left-hand bank ahead of him. That he figured was a boathouse, and he was right.

He kept in so close now that he almost touched the low, grassy bank, and in this fashion he paddled on until he suddenly saw the stone bulk of the three-arched bridge loom up just ahead of him. Once through there he knew the river made an abrupt turn and divided, forming a miniature island of mud and rushes.

If he could manoeuvre on the right-hand side of this island he would stand a chance of missing any houseboats that might be moored there, for he knew that in days gone by they were usually moored in the left-hand channel.

He found things had not changed. He caught a glimpse of first one, then a second and a third, but they were in the other channel, and when he was midway through the other stretch of water he lost sight of them entirely. Then he was in a broader bit of stream, and he knew that another half-mile would bring him to the creek, partly natural and partly artificial, that led along to the paddocks, belonging to the house which was his objective.

As he came round another bend in the stream he suddenly saw

several oblongs of light away to his left. He stopped paddling for a moment until he assured himself they must be the windows of the houses on the creek. Then he laughed softly.

"That letter has done the trick," he muttered, beginning to paddle once more. "The poor fish is sitting there with the fear of Hades in him and every light on, like some silly woman afraid of the dark, or I miss my guess very badly. And they call him a crook of some calibre! Faugh! The breed has degenerated since the days when I was last in England."

He was nearing the creek now, and by the feel of the paddle in the water he could tell that the inrush of the tide had just about stopped. In a few minutes it would be racing out at high speed; he must finish matters and take advantage of it.

The mouth of the creek was broad and easy to negotiate. Once round the bend it was almost still water, and a few minutes steady paddling brought him to a little rustic bridge. He stopped here, got out, and lifted the light craft after him. Leaving this on the edge in the shadow of the bridge, he started ahead on foot.

At first Plummer was inclined to walk boldly up to the door and ring the bell. He was deterred from that by the thought that if the man within was in a bad state of funk he might begin shooting from some point which, commanded the front porch. Then, too, he might count on the sight of all the lights making anyone approaching the place believe that several persons were inside.

So Plummer made his way round to the back of the house, wondering as he went if he were being observed. He was not challenged. On that side the windows were alight as in the front. This rather complicated matters, for he knew it was now hopeless to make a surreptitious entry. He must strike boldly.

He did so. Turning aside from the path, he made straight for one of the lower windows. Standing close to the sill he tried to force it up, finding, as he had anticipated, that it was locked. But there was a light in the room, which he took to be either dining-room or study, so quite coolly he lifted his hand and tapped loudly.

He jumped as the blind flew up and the sash followed. So abrupt was the action he knew that his movements must have been under surveillance from the moment he began to walk towards the house. At first he could not see the person who had worked the blind and jerked the sash high, but in the next moment he saw a man seated at a desk, a heavy automatic pistol in his hand, and on the right of the window another man, dressed in the sober black of a manservant.

George Marsden Plummer grinned. He had drawn no weapon, and now, ignoring the menace of the other, he climbed over the sill. He was going on the old and well-proved theory that if a man doesn't shoot on the first threat he isn't likely to shoot at all in cold blood. Those few moments' hesitation were to cost the man who called himself John Dean, his life, although he didn't know it yet. The weak point in his armour was that he didn't know whether this visitor of the night was friend or foe.

Plummer ignored the manservant, and, turning coolly, closed the window and drew the blind. During those moments his back was turned to the gaping mouth of the heavy automatic, and it would have been well for John Dean had he shot then. But the man was completely baffled by this cool stranger. He hesitated and lost the game.

When Plummer turned again, he lifted one hand.

"Put your weapon away, John Dean," he said easily. "Or lay it on the desk if you prefer. I have some things to say to you—alone. It will pay you to listen to me."

Slowly, reluctantly, dominated by the other's manner, Dean obeyed. He put the pistol on the desk, and made a gesture of dismissal to the man, who all this time had remained motionless by the window. The fellow went as if he didn't like the affair at all; and the moment the door closed after him he had his proof.

For, like a flash, Plummer jerked out his own small but deadly automatic, and, before John Dean could get his fingers within three inches of his own weapon, Plummer had sent a bullet into his skull, a little above, and exactly midway between the eyes. George Marsden Plummer was one of the most deadly and cold-blooded "killers" who had over been let loose on society.

The small hole that appeared told him all he wanted to know. He did not pause to investigate further, but, turning, raced for the door. The other crook who had been posing as the manservant was already running along the hall when Plummer jerked open the door. Plummer took after him, and up the front stairs they went two at a time.

On the first floor the fugitive turned to the left, making for the back of the house, where he probably hoped to escape by the rear staircase. It was just at the top of the flight that Plummer caught up with him. There the other turned at bay. Plummer did not shoot. He had already jammed his weapon back into his pocket, and now he threw his mighty arms about his victim.

For the second time since being in England he brought into play the deadly hold that he had learned in the Rif. There was a brief straining, a hoarse cry, and then something went bumping down the stairs, to fall in a huddled heap at the bottom.

Twenty minutes later, George Marsden Plummer stole forth from that house of death, leaving every light burning as he had found it, and the front door slightly ajar, in a spirit of cynical humour. It is one of the little things that will puzzle the police, he had thought to himself; let them worry over it.

In those twenty minutes he had stripped the two bodies clean of all that was on them, and placed on the neck of each the brand of wei-len-pung. He carried away the letter he had written to John Dean; and in an inner pocket reposed two more of the sacred Five Pearl Thimbles of Chen-tse.

He had worked well on behalf of the woman who had caught him up into the white-hot blast of her meteoric passage across the firmament of crime and passion.

It was George Marsden Plummer who appeared later in the day as Henry Dean, when Sexton Blake and Inspector Thomas of Scotland Yard were beginning an investigation of the mysterious double murder at the house on the creek. It says much for his disguise that not for a single moment did Sexton Blake suspect his identity; and no eye was keener than Blake's to pierce a disguise.

His get away had been simple enough. In the same little rubber craft he had used before, he drifted down on the tide until he was just above Arundel. There he had landed, and, after deflating his boat, had made his way up through the heavily wooded park adjoining the famous castle to the road where the two-seater was waiting.

Back to London they had driven by a roundabout way, being nearly halfway to the metropolis when Constable Tarrant's curiosity was aroused by the lighted windows of the house on the creek.

It suited the same evil quirk of Plummer's humour to pay his accomplice with the money he had taken from Sam Danvers' pockets, and that afternoon he had travelled down to Houghton quite openly by train. He was perfectly well aware that he was under the surveillance of the police all the time he remained in the house, but Plummer was puzzled about the whereabouts of the other pearl.

He could account for four up to now. As he figured things, John Dean should have had two in his possession. He had found only one, however, and one on the person of the man he had hurled down the stairs. If the fourth gem wasn't in that house, where was it? Was the demented Chinaman in Paris the only person who held that secret?

He resolved to remain until after the inquest in order to make his search, but, though he raked that house from one end to the other, from cellar to garret, he found nothing.

When the inquest was over, Plummer faded away at the exact moment he chose. In the early hours of the morning he prepared his little rubber craft, and once more floated down the Arun as the tide raced seawards, right under the noses of the police who were posted about the district.

Thus ran the sequence of events that preceded the arrival of Sexton Blake on the scene. But, clever as he had been, Plummer was not to discover, until he reached Paris, just what use Sexton Blake had made of those few days following the murders!

AND what of Blake?

Needless to say, Tinker was aghast at Blake's sudden collapse. He had seen by the beading sweat on Blake's forehead that his master was undergoing a terrific strain; but the swiftness of the breakdown came as something almost beyond anything he had ever known of Blake.

In the crisis which now faced him he forgot about Fu Won Chang. He did not even know that the latter had somehow contrived to get hold of the two imitation pearls, which Blake had used as a magnet in his efforts to bring the Chinaman out of the state into which his mind had been thrown; he did not see that Fu Won Chang was fondling the two spheres in an awed and yet contented manner. All Tinker had sense or care for was his prone master.

Into the midst of this hurly-burly came the superintendent, accompanied by no less a person that M. Dupuis, the prefect of police. On being driven from the room by Blake, the former had deemed it his duty to get through, on the telephone to the prefect. Blake's permit covered a good deal, but, to his mind, it did not entitle the Englishman to treat him as if he were "cochon," and to act as if the institution were his own private establishment.

Therefore he had screamed to M. Dupuis that the mad Englishman was killing his Chinese patient, and would M. Dupuis please come at once to the place.

M. Dupuis, knowing perfectly well what Blake was attempting to do, came not to appease the superintendent's piqued vanity, but to make sure that he did not further interfere with Blake's experiment. And when he saw the condition of things that existed, he lost no time in revealing that immense efficiency which had made him one of the ablest men who have ever been at the Paris Surete.

He grasped the situation without need for explanation from Tinker. In the next moment he was assisting Tinker in his efforts to revive his master, and when Blake's lids fluttered and then opened, he heaved just as big a sigh of relief.

Blake sat up, his face showing deep chagrin as he realised what had happened.

"Stupid of me," he muttered, pushing away their restraining

hands and scrambling to his feet. "And you, cher ami, how did you get here?"

M. Dupuis thought it wiser not to reveal the crass idiocy of his subordinate, so he simply explained that he thought he would come on and see how the experiment was progressing; then, for the first time, his eyes really embraced the Chinaman. As they did so his jaw dropped in amazement.

"Why—why—" he stammered.

Blake smiled wearily.

"Yes, it is true, monsieur. He has come back, and he will not return to the land of shadows."

"But, dear friend, this is a miracle! Our best men have said that his mind was shattered utterly; that nothing would ever mend the damage."

"And they should have been right had it not been that the major part of the trouble was psychological, produced by a certain form of hypnotism that is exceedingly rare in the West. But I shall explain matters later, monsieur. What I wish now is to get away and, with your permission, to take this poor wretch with me. I know there are certain formalities, but I want you to dispense with them. I shall be bond for him in any way you wish."

"Is it urgent, M. Blake?"

"It is urgent. If you will do me the honour to come to my hotel with me I shall lay before you my hypothesis of this case. There is much to do before this night is over, and a great deal depends on how far Fu Won Chang can help us."

At the sound of his own name, the Chinaman paused in his play with the two imitation pearls, and gazed at Blake. Then, suddenly, he sprang to his feet and caught hold of Blake's hands. Lifting them, he placed the backs against his forehead, bending in complete submission as he did so.

It was an extraordinary thing for a high-caste Manchu to do. Then he poured out a flood of Chinese that even Blake found it difficult to follow. The gist of it was that Fu Won Chang was placing himself— his life and all that might be his now or in the hereafter at the service of this man who had brought his soul back to him. Where it had been for those weeks—what had happened to him he had no idea.

All he could guess was that something terrible had overtaken him, and, later on, when he remembered the torture that had caused it, would come the greatest risk of a relapse. That was one reason why Blake wanted to keep him close to his influence until the crisis was over—so that he could be there to meet it and beat back the devils of horror in that last attack.

Thus it befell that when Blake, Tinker and M. Dupuis drove away from the place, Fu Won Chang went with them.

Time and again it has been revealed, in so far as a mere recorder of events could reveal, how Sexton Blake's mind worked when engaged on a particular problem. But not even Blake himself could have explained just how he sorted out the various items that he considered important enough to be listed mentally and brought them into a common point of focus.

The broad principles on which he worked were based on the same system —that system which he himself had devised; but his analysis of each case was what decided him on exactly what way those principles should be applied. He had brought the science of crime analysis and detection down to a finer point than any other living criminologist.

He was not ruled by any one dogma; he had a catholic conception of other sciences bearing on that in which he specialised, and he had always been ready to take from each anything that might be of benefit to him. It was this breadth of outlook that had contributed greatly to his success, and it was because he was quick to discard any worn-out theory in favour of any new discovery, that he kept himself in the forefront of his profession.

It was for that reason he had left others far behind and likewise why his services were sought by high and low. It was a common phrase to hear that if a case could not be solved, Sexton Blake was the man to solve it—rather an Irish way of saying that in the line of crime detection Sexton Blake would find a solution if one existed.

It was for these reasons that Blake had been able to meet and control the peculiar features surrounding the case on which he was at present engaged. Before making his decision to seek a solution in Paris he had covered a great deal of ground by analyses bringing each part of the whole down to a common denominator, so to say.

And it was because he arrived each time at a common base that he finally made up his mind the solution lay through Fu Won Chang—if solution there were. But Fu Won Chang was mentally incapable; if he possessed any secret it had been lost in the great void into which his functioning senses had been plunged by the devilish work of the priests of Chen-tse.

Then how could he reach into those deeps and pull out the answer to his problem?

Only by bringing back to sanity that soul and mind which were wandering Heaven only knew where.

It was a gigantic task; it was a thing which only a master of the most subtle forms of Eastern psychology would have dared to tackle; and it needed a super-will to bolster up that knowledge. Sexton Blake had put himself to the test, and he had succeeded. Could he now make use of the material he had picked out of the spiritual cosmos?

Back in his sitting-room at the Carlitz when Fu Won Chang had been given a strong nerve sedative; Blake took out certain papers from his bag and laid them on the table. Next he opened the dossier which Inspector Journet had brought him, covering what was known by the French police of the past and present of Vali Mata-Vali.

Then, working from one to the other, he began to speak in low tones, laying before M. Dupuis the whole theory he had worked out regarding the Five Sacred Pearl Thimbles of Chen-tse.

It was a revelation that caused that able police official to open his eyes; and it took a good deal to impress M. Dupuis. The prefect had served a long apprenticeship under Dr. Lafarge, in the famous French police laboratories at Lyons.

But he did not interrupt during the whole course of the exposition of ideas except to shrug repeatedly and ejaculate an explosive "tiens!" or "parbleu!" All this time Fu Won Chang was sitting tranquilly rubbing the two imitation pearls in his hand. Not once did he remove his gaze from Blake's countenance, although he understood nothing of what was being said. Now and then he would recognise such words as "Buddha," "Chen-tse," and others of his own language; but that was all.

Yet when Blake finished and M. Dupuis broke into a torrent of words in French, Fu Won Chang's eyes lit with sudden interest, for this was a language he understood. He could tell little of what the prefect was speaking of, but in some way he gathered that it had to do with him, and he kept gazing earnestly from one to the other.

"It is, as I said, a miracle, monsieur," the prefect was exclaiming. "You have outlined a wonderful theory. But how to prove it?"

It was then the Celestial knew that it all had something to do with him, for he heard Blake say:

"I am going to try and prove it through Fu Won Chang."

''Mais—comment, monsieur?"

.   .   .   .   .

"Je vous dirai, monsieur le prefect. Figurez-vous—"

And so Blake laid out his scheme. When he was finished the prefect nodded his grey head in approval.

"It is the plan of an artist, monsieur; but—"

"Wait, please."

Then Blake turned to Fu Won Chang. As he began to speak in Cantonese, M. Dupuis and Tinker bent forward to listen intently; the Celestial kept his eyes glued on Blake's. Slowly Blake sketched out the story of what he thought had happened in the affairs of Fu Won Chang from the moment that misguided Celestial had braved the terrors of the holy of holies of the Temple of Eternal Purity and had managed to get away with the Five Pearl Thimbles of Chen-tse.

He continued with a relation of what he thought Fu had done with some of the pearls after he had sailed from Hong Kong, but he spoke as if he knew all this for fact.

Then he dwelt on Fu's hectic and meteoric career in the French capital, finishing with his seizure by the priests of Chen-tse on the night he had returned to his quarters to get one of the pearls for Vali Mata-Vali. And there he paused to ask a question.

"Is not all this the truth, Fu Won Chang?" he asked gently. "Is it not as the powers have given me to know?"

"Honourable one, you speak as one who saw all. I cannot. I cannot lie to you; for your words have made me remember. I—"

He broke off as a shudder tore him from head to foot. The sudden recollection of something terrible during that time of torture had caused an upheaval within him. But Blake had been watching for just such a thing, and was quick to counter it.

Like a flash he was round the table, one arm lying firmly across Fu's thin shoulders. Soothingly he talked to him until the Celestial looked up into his eyes trustfully. Blake's control was greater than the dread of those terrible days. It was proof of how completely his will had cleansed the mind of the other.

"You are quite safe, quite safe, Fu," he said again and again. "Those priests of Chen-tse can never harm you again. You can trust me in every way. I mean you nothing but good; and this other honourable friend is far more powerful than all the priests of Chen-tse combined. He rules all this great city, and I have his faithful word that no harm shall come to you. But you have done a great wrong, Fu. It was not only a sin to your own faith that you took away the sacred Thimbles of Chen-tse; your sinning has involved others. You must make restitution as far as is in your power, and with your help I can see that this is done. Never will you be able to return to your own country until this is done, and in only one way can it be accomplished. Will you trust me?"

Fu caught his hand.

"Honourable one, thou art to me as my most sacred ancestor. I shall obey in all ways after which, if it is thy will, I shall assume the yellow cord." (This meant suicide after the Chinese fashion.)

"It will not be necessary for you to take the yellow cord, Fu. But you must do all you can to help. There are certain questions you must answer."

"Honourable one, I am thy slave."

"You were seized by the priests of Chen-tse, as I have said?"

"It is so."

"We shall not dwell on what happened to you there. That is done with. But I must know some things. When you were seized you were on your way to this woman of the theatre?"

"It is so."

"You had with you one of the Pearl Thimbles of Chen-tse?"

"You have named it, honourable one."

"You had given away three on the ship after leaving Hong Kong?"

"Three, as thou hast said, honourable one, in order to buy safety."

"Then there was another, Fu. Where was that fifth pearl on the night you were seized by the priests of Chen-tse?"

"Among my private belongings, honourable one."

Blake turned quickly to the prefect. "Can you tell me, monsieur, what happened to his private effects?"

"They will be, of course, at the prefecture."

"A thorough search was made?"

"Naturally."

"Then if the pearl he says was among them had been there it would have been found."

"Mais, oui."

102

"Can you tell me, monsieur, if the woman, Vali Mata-Vali, was allowed access to his rooms after his disappearance?"

Monsieur Dupuis thumped the table. "But how stupid of me! Of course, mon ami. I distinctly remember. Besides, it was Mademoiselle Vali Mata-Vali who gave certain information to the police after he was found wandering in the Bois."

"Yes; I hadn't thought of that. It would have been quite possible then for Mademoiselle Vali Mata-Vali to have made a search of his effects before anyone else. I think that explains matters. Unless I am mistaken in my whole hypothesis of the affair, then Mademoiselle Vali Mata-Vali is in possession of that pearl as well as the others. All but the one which the priests secured."

"You do think, then, my friend, that the woman has some connection with those murders which you are investigating?"

"Who else but she or the priests of Chen-tse? Each of the victims bore the mark of 'wei-len-pung,' monsieur. It is the mark of the priests, it is true; but—I don't know. There are other factors that make me believe the woman is mixed up in it, either as an accomplice of the priests or in some other way. Her movements are suspicious. Why did she go off to Morocco? Why did she return so unobtrusively? She is a mystery woman, monsieur, and I believe that when we have solved the riddle she represents we shall know more—much more of the matter."

Blake returned again to Fu Won Chang.

"Do you know to what place you were taken by the priests of Chen-tse?"

"It is not known to me, honourable one."

"If they are still in Paris I can locate them," broke in M. Dupuis. "Inspector Journet is the man for that job. He knows the Chinese quarter intimately. He can go through every hole in it."

"Could that be arranged at once, monsieur?"

"You mean this evening?"

"Yes."

"I can put Journet on the job as soon as I leave here. I guarantee he will run your priests to earth inside two hours."

"Good! Then here is my plan, monsieur."

Blake spoke earnestly for some minutes, during which the prefect and Tinker listened closely. Then when he had finished he put into Chinese for Fu's benefit what he had been saying to the others. At first the Celestial showed distinct signs of nerves, but when Blake assured him that he would be beside him each moment he finally consented.

As a matter of fact, the Manchu would have trusted himself to any test had Blake demanded it. And yet Blake would have given much had it not been necessary to put the poor wreck of a creature through any further trial. What he needed was a long period of complete rest, and Blake had determined inwardly that he should have it just as soon as this case was over.

But he was equally determined to secure the Five Pearl Thimbles of Chen-tse for his client and friend, Hong-Lo-Soo. It didn't matter two straws to Blake whether he had to take one or more away from the priests of Chen-tse in order to do so, even though he knew that it was Hong-Lo-Soo's intention to return them to the temple in Canton.

He had said to Hong-Lo-Soo in London that the treatment meted out to Fu Won Chang had been beyond all excuse, and now he was more convinced than ever of this. But he was anxious, too, that there should be a clearing up of the part played by Vali Mata-Vali in the affair, for Blake was strongly of the opinion that a party of Chinese priests could not have made their way into England, carried out a triple murder, and then got clear again so quickly. That was the strongest reason that made him think they had not actually committed those three murders.

Then who had done so? he kept on asking himself. Had Vali Mata-Vali had a hand in that phase of it? And if so, had her mysterious journey to Morocco anything to do with it? Blake frankly confessed to himself that it was one of the most baffling cases he had had on the boards for a long time.

But he was risking all on the hypothesis he had formed as a result of his deductions from the few scraps of evidence available. And what he had been able to learn in Paris as well as what he had confirmed through Fu Won Chang only strengthened his theory. That night would prove whether he was on the right track or not.

There was no time to be lost, for there was much to be done. Soon after Blake had outlined his proposals, Monsieur Dupuis took his departure, promising to put Inspector Journet on the trail of the priests of Chen-tse without delay. He also was to place a special detail of a dozen plain-clothes detectives at Blake's orders for the whole night, the inspector in charge to report to Blake at the Folies Bergere.

For not only was Blake still planning to go to that abode of frivolity, but he intended taking Fu Won Chang along with him, and Tinker. To this end there were several things to be done. Blake had decided that Fu Won Chang must make an appearance as nearly like what he had been as possible. He himself had determined to assume the disguise of a mandarin of the purple button, while Tinker was to appear as a Chinese of the type one sees among the students of Paris.

Through Monsieur Dupuis' card to the director of the Folies Bergere they were assured of a private stage box and access to any part of the theatre that Blake might wish to penetrate should it become necessary.

Tinker was sent out with a full list of requirements to a certain shop in the Avenue de l'Opera where Chinese merchandise was stocked; from there he was to go on to the Folies as he drove back, and hand in the prefect's card to the director of the theatre.

In the meantime, Blake directed himself to Fu Won Chang, and, once they were alone, the Celestial strove mightily to give Blake every scrap of information he could. By the time Tinker returned, Blake had learned quite a lot more of some value regarding the Five Pearl Thimbles of Chen-tse, and his hopes were beating high that before the night was out he would be able to lay his hands on the gems.

If he succeeded in doing so it would be no little triumph, for Blake did not disguise from himself the fact that he was beset on every side by sinister and utterly ruthless forces.

There could be no doubt about the popularity of "la belle Vali" among the Parisians, for that evening the theatre was packed as it had been since her return. The show at the Folies Bergere is, of course, a variety affair, sometimes faintly reminiscent of a review in which a thin plot runs through the whole piece as a theme, or, again, it may be composed of entirely separate displays, the chief ingredients of which are plenty of girls scantily attired, and a profusion of colour in the lights and stage dressing.

Such was it on this night, when three very richly dressed Chinese entered a stage box and seated themselves a little space back from the padded edge.

The "turn" which was the feature of the show, and was that in which Mademoiselle Vali Mata-Vali appeared, was a wonderful symphony of Oriental colour and subtle lighting. In it, "la belle Vali " danced in a way that had never been seen, even in Paris, until she came; and there was no doubt that, as an artiste, she was supreme.

It is no part of this record to give a detailed account of the various numbers which preceded her appearance. They went off in the usual manner, and it was immediately after the interval that Vali Mata-Vali came on. During the first part of her dance the theatre was in almost complete darkness, while the stage lights were induced to a minimum.

The colouring was jade green—the shade which Vali favoured above all others. It was when the dance increased in passionate abandon that the lights increased slowly, the light being gauged to reach a blazing zenith when she should have risen to the ultimate point of the dance.

So it went on this night—the whirling, dipping, tantalising, supple figure, outlined exotically against a background that suggested the increasing and storming fury of the whole thing, until the light came to a high pitch and she whirled to a last dizzy crescendo of perfect motion until—she found herself gazing straight into the eyes of Fu Won Chang, who could almost have reached out of the stage-box and touched her.

The woman paused as if frozen in her tracks. The audience, thinking this was the end of the dance, fairly rose to its feet in thunderous applause. Somehow, she dragged her eyes away from Fu Won Chang, and for a moment they met the deep, satirical orbs of his companion—a stern-faced Celestial in the embroidered tunic of a mandarin of the purple button. Then she was bowing mechanically to the cheering audience, while an attendant was handing up several bouquets of gorgeous flowers.

Normally, la belle Vali would have given an encore, but now when she bowed her way from the stage, the curtain descended, and, despite the continuance of hand-clapping and cheering, she did not reappear. When it was plain that she would not do so, the tall mandarin rose and whispered a word or two in the ear of Fu Won Chang.

He then approached the door of the box, followed by the youth who had been seated beside him. As he opened the door, two men in dark suits hurried forward, and the mandarin made a gesture towards Fu Won Chang.

"Come into the box and remain out of sight," he ordered in French. "Do not leave him a single moment, and permit no one to enter under any pretext. I shall return presently."

With that he hurried along the corridor, closely followed by the youth. A door, a little way along, gave access to another passage which was private to the employees of the theatre. A man was on duty here, but when the tall Celestial showed him a card, signed by the director, he and his companion were permitted to pass.

They almost ran until they came to another door, which, on being opened, let them directly out into the narrow passage at the back of the theatre. Blake, for it was he, was about to step out, his objective being the stage-door, when he drew back suddenly and, standing with the door open just a few inches, watched.

Hurrying down the passage came Vali Mata-Vali. She must have changed in record time, and, indeed, as she drew nearer, both Blake and Tinker could see that she had not waited to remove all her make-up. With her was a tall man, to whom she was talking in low, excited tones, and the moment his features came beneath the light, Sexton Blake lost all immediate interest in the woman.

For the man was he who had arrived at the house on the creek, near Arundel, when Blake was there, and had given his name as Henry Dean. It was the man who, according to Inspector Thomas, had disappeared immediately after the inquest.

CHAPTER 13. Blake Moves.

NOR was that all.

Almost in the same instant those keen eyes of Blake's, sharpened by suspicion now, as they had not been sharpened at the house on the creek, bored through the disguise of the man, and recognised the identity of the master criminal beneath —George Marsden Plummer.

That was enough. Now he knew there could be no doubt that Vali Mata-Vali was deeply mixed up in the affair; now he knew why she had taken that mysterious journey to Morocco. Now he knew that, not a dozen yards from him walked the man who had killed that other crook, known as John Dean—the lesser criminal who had posed as the manservant, Caleb Peters —the ex-lag, Sam Danvers.

But what had Plummer to do with the priests of Chen-tse? That there was some strong bond between them was certain, from the fact that each victim had been branded with the wei-lun-pung mark. The secret of that brand could only come from the priests of Chen-tse. Was that connection just another puzzle that could be explained through the woman? Who was Vali Mata-Vali?

Blake had no time for more than to give a passing thought to those questions. The main issue was to run that pair to their lair and strike before it was too late. His play of getting Fu Won Chang into the stage box, where the dancer must see him at some part or another of her piece, had resulted exactly as he had hoped. Her sudden frozen horror at the sight of the Celestial sitting there perfectly sane and tranquil, when, according to all accounts he was a raving maniac, had stripped the mask from her long enough for Blake to read the truth, but he had not counted on the other; he had not dreamed that George Marsden Plummer was the missing factor for which he was seeking.

And he knew at once the woman told Plummer what had happened, that wily criminal would soon sense the something threatening that lay behind Fu's appearance in the stage box. To suspect, with Plummer, was to take to flight. Hence if Blake were to strike at all, he must be quick.

Well was it for Blake then that he had taken the precaution to ask M. Dupuis for a special detail of men. By the time Plummer and Vali Mata-Vali had reached the end of the passage, where a big limousine car was waiting, Blake was able to step out without being seen, and swiftly he sent a signal that should be picked up by at least one of the men who was on watch. That signal meant:

"Follow the two persons who are just coming out of the passage, and report by telephone to the theatre as soon as possible."

Then he stepped back into the building, and, after a low-toned conversation with Tinker, led the way back to where he had left Fu Won Chang. Blake found the Celestial seated just as he had been, with the two men on guard in the shadow at the back of the box.

The show was still in progress, and, since there was nothing to be done now but wait until he heard from Inspector Journet, and the man to whom he had just signalled, he made a pretence of watching the stage, although he was chafing inwardly with a fierce impatience.

Sexton Blake would have found more satisfaction in laying George Marsden Plummer by the heels than almost any living criminal. And now there was before him a chance such as he had not had for years.

He was not to be kept waiting long, however. M. Dupuis had made no vain boast when he said that Inspector Journet was the man to dig up the hiding-place of the priests of Chen-tse. The particular display that had been in progress when Blake returned to the box was not yet finished, when there came a tap at the door, and Journet thrust his head in. With a sign to Tinker to remain where he was, Blake got up and joined the inspector in the corridor.

"Are you ready, Monsieur Blake?" asked Journet, with a smile. He had been told how Blake would be disguised, but he had not seen him before that evening.

"Your question means you have succeeded."

"But, yes, monsieur. I was given the job to do. Tiens! One cannot waste time over yellow figureheads."

Blake laughed. The other was a little vain, but it was harmless.

"I think we had better go on at once, then. I want my assistant to come, but our Chinois friend—"

"You wish to keep him safely. That's easy, M. Blake. I can send him on to the prefecture with two of my men. He will be safe enough there."

"Good! And, what is more, he will not be frightened. I—But wait a moment, M. Journet. Here comes your colleague with one of his men. I think it possible they have something else to report."

Inspector Collet, the man who had been sent in charge of the special force from the Surete, came up at that moment, and, after nodding to Journet, turned to Blake.

"This man, monsieur," he said, indicating his companion, "caught your signal. He followed the car in which Mademoiselle Vali Mata-Vali and her companion drove off. They went to mademoiselle's private house—an old chateau in St. Cloud. The car was afterwards driven over the drawbridge at the rear, and it is presumed that mademoiselle and her companion intend remaining within for the present, at least."

"A drawbridge! Is there, then, a moat?"

"Oui, monsieur."

"Is it dry or filled with water?"

"It is as it has always been, monsieur—about five metres of water."

Blake turned back to Journet.

"I think it will be necessary for me to go first to the place where the priests are lurking. It is in Montparnasse?"

"Yes, monsieur."

"And you, Monsieur Collet, can you get your men together at once, and go to St. Cloud?"

"We can start within a few minutes, monsieur. Is it the chateau?"

"Yes. Can you surround it, or, at least, post your men at several vantage points? Inspector Journet and I have another visit to make first. I think we should arrive at the chateau in about an hour and a half, or two hours."

"Of a surety, monsieur. But if mademoiselle and her companion leave the place before you come?"

"Then have them followed, please. If they get away before we turn up I shall have to think of another plan; but, at any cost, monsieur, do not permit them to get away from the Paris area, even if you have to make an arrest."

"You can depend on me, monsieur." Inspector Collet detailed two of his men to take Fu Won Chang on to the prefecture. The Celestial was loath to go, and it was only after Blake had given him his personal assurance that he would be safe, that he consented.

Blake would have been able to play a stronger hand had he been in a position to take Fu along with him, but he knew that the poor fellow was not equal to much more nerve strain that night, and he hadn't the heart to push him too far. It had been a good deal that he had been able to face the stage as he had done. And, after all, Blake had a card of his own to play with the priests of Chen-tse which he counted on being strong enough to take the trick.

Then Inspector Collet disappeared, and, as soon as he was gone, Blake, Tinker, Inspector Journet, and three specials, who were accompanying the inspector, climbed into a police motorcar, and headed at top speed for the left bank of the river.

Journet had run his quarry to earth in much the same way that Plummer had found them. It had not been really difficult once he had got into the quarter, and as they entered the dark cul-de-sac, a man stepped out of the shadow to inform his superior that they were still "at home."

Blake asked that the three specials should be left on guard in the cul-de-sac, and that, until their business was over, the place should be closed to anyone passing in or out, unless Vali Mata-Vali and her companions should show up. Blake had an idea that this was a possibility, though he did not think it very likely.

Then he and Tinker followed Journet up flight after flight of stairs until they reached the third floor of the rat-ridden old building. There Journet rapped authoritatively on a door, and, without waiting for an answer, threw his shoulder against it.

It had been bolted on the inside, but it flew in quickly enough under that assault, and the three stood on the threshold gazing at the three wizened Orientals who were standing in a group by the table, obviously on the point of leaving the room. And a sudden instinct told Sexton Blake whither they had been bound.

It was now up to him to take control, so Journet, no little interested to watch the English detective at work, fell back. Tinker moved ahead with Blake, while three pairs of wise, old eyes went from one to the other. Then Blake bowed formally, uttering a few words of conventional greeting. The priests replied, but gave him no lead. Nor did Blake require one.

Stepping close to the table, he put out one long finger, and slowly made an imaginary drawing on the wood top which was the private tong cipher of Hong-Lo-Soo, most exalted of all men in the tongs of the Four Lakes and Three Feathers.

Dead silence followed, while the three pairs of sloe-coloured eyes stared at him in an awed way. Then Blake spoke again.

"I am come from the exalted one, whose cipher you have seen, to complete the work you have done so badly. I am come as the blood brother and personal representative of the exalted Hong-Lo-Soo, who says that the mulberry tree will wither before you bring your visit to a finish. You have acted as suckling babes—you, who are the wise men of the Temple of Eternal Purity. You have shattered him who was the original sinner in the desecration of the Five Pearl Thimbles of Buddha; and what have you gained? I will answer for you. You have gained but one of those sacred Thimbles. Where are the others? I will again answer. They are in the possession of a dog of an unbeliever. And you, the wise men of the temple, the keepers of the secred ark, have had dealings with this one of evil. Answer me; is it not so?"

"It is so, exalted one," returned the eldest of the trio, in a quavering voice.

Who this tall, commanding stranger might be, none of the three could guess; but he came with the knowledge of the private cipher of the exalted Hong-Lo-Soo, and that was enough.

"You were leaving as I came in," went on Blake, pressing his advantage home. "I see with the eyes of one who stands on the mountain top. I shall tell you. You were going to this one of evil. Is it not so?"

"It is so, exalted one."

"For what purpose? To receive the Four Pearl Thimbles of Chen-tse? Or to give up the one you have?"

"The four have been promised, exalted one. We were but to go, and receive them."

"And in return you were to give— what?"

"The treasure of the Forty Moons!"

"Ah!"

The treasure of the Forty Moons! Well did Sexton Blake know what that meant. It might be but a minor treasure of the Temple of Eternal Purity, but in cold terms of the West it was a collection of magnificent diamonds worth almost anything one might care to name. So this was what George Marsden Plummer was to receive for handing over the remaining Four Pearl Thimbles of Chen-tse.

"You brought to this country the treasure of the Forty Moons?"

"It was necessary, exalted one, to have the wherewithal with which to bargain if an opportunity came; also, money would be needed."

"Know you that this one of evil killed thrice to get possession of the thimbles?"

"A human life is but a breath, exalted one; the sacred Thimbles of Chen-tse shine for ever."

So he was right, after all, thought Blake; Plummer was the man who had done the triple murder in England.

"The methods of the East are not the methods of the West," he said coldly. "And the exalted Hong-Lo-Soo is displeased. I am come to complete this work. You will give me the treasure of the Forty Moons. I shall deal with it as I deem best."

So completely had he impressed the priests that, without a moment's hesitation, one of them took out a heavy bag from beneath his tunic and handed it across. Blake took it and gave it to Tinker.

A conservative estimate of the value of the contents of that bag would be, Blake knew, not less than half a million pounds. And when it had been handed over to Plummer, the latter would be free to deal with the diamonds as he wished, without the slightest risk of interference. It would be, in a way a free gift. The game he and Vali Mata-Vali had been playing was clear enough now, and Blake had to confess to himself that it was one of no mean calibre.

"How do you know where to find this one of evil?" he asked abruptly.

For answer, the senior priest drew out a slip of paper and laid it on the table. Blake bent over it and read in pencilled, block letters the address of the chateau in St. Cloud where Vali Mata-Vali and Plummer had been trailed by Inspector Collet. He folded it and put it inside his own tunic.

"We shall keep the appointment," he said briefly. "The Pearl Thimbles of Chen-tse must be recovered. You, wise one, will do the taking, as was planned. I shall be known as the keeper of the treasure of the Forty Moons. Is it understood?"

"We obey, exalted one."

"You will proceed as if I had not come. You will make your bargain with this one of evil, and at the moment I shall place the treasure of the Forty Moons before him. Then I shall act. Make no error, wise men of the temple, or you will answer for it with"—and here Blake bent forward to whisper—"the mark of 'wei-len-pung.' "

They shrank back at the terrible threat, and a few moments later, when he shepherded them out of the room, Blake knew they would do his bidding. With this addition to the party they motored to St. Cloud, and just before reaching the chateau Blake, Tinker, and the three priests went ahead on foot.

"Follow slowly," said Blake to Inspector Journet. "Find Collet and watch the drawbridge. If these priests are expected, it will be down. And exactly five minutes after we disappear within do you and Collet come after us with some of your men; but leave some on guard outside. I do not know what room we shall be in; you must find it. But do not wait longer than the five minutes."

Then he strode away, and instead of three Celestials crossing the drawbridge, as Plummer and Vali Mata-Vali expected, there were five persons clad in Oriental robes who sought admission,

The chateau—at one time one of the strongest of the minor castles in the Paris region—was an extensive pile surrounded, as Collet had said, by a moat. It was fully fifty feet wide, and from what the inspector had told them, Blake and Tinker knew it was not less than three metres deep.

The main drawbridge was down, and when they had been examined by a manservant they were permitted to pass. Farther down, Blake could just make out another erection that he took to be the secondary drawbridge of which Collet had spoken, and something made him wonder in that moment if Journet would think to place a guard there.

Then they were in a courtyard, and a little later another man admitted them to a wide, stone-flagged hall. They were conducted along this to a door at the far end. Their guide paused and rapped, and Blake heard a voice, which he recognised as Plummer's, bid them enter.

The next moment they were in a bizarre room, most luxuriously furnished, where Vali Mata-Vali half reclined on a wide divan. Plummer had evidently been pacing up and down, for he was standing in the centre of the room, as if he had just come to a pause. And Blake noticed, too, that they were wearing the outer coats which they had worn when leaving the theatre. It looked to the detective as if they were ready to clear out as soon as the deal was completed.

Plummer came forward and motioned the manservant to leave the room. He looked searchingly at Blake and Tinker, but their disguises defied his gaze. Perhaps if he had not been so anxious to get on with the business he might have been more suspicious; but he turned to the old man who had previously acted as spokesman, and, addressing him in his broken Cantonese, said curtly:

"You have brought the diamonds?"

The old man made a gesture in Blake's direction.

"The keeper of the treasure of the Forty Moons has it in his care, honourable one. And thou hast the sacred Thimbles of Chen-tse?"

"I have them. Let us to our bargain. To you I shall hand the Four Thimbles of Chen-tse, O Wise One. Is it agreed?"

"It is agreed."

"And thou shalt hand to me the treasure of the Forty Moons."

"It is agreed."

"I receive your promise on the foot of the sacred Buddha that it is the treasure of the Forty Moons and nothing else?"

"It is agreed."

"There is one thing more, O Wise One!"

"My unworthy ears await your words, honourable one."

Plummer bent forward.

"Some years ago," he said slowly, "one of the girls of the Temple of Eternal Purity was—lost. It is said that she was drowned in the river in Canton. Do you recall that, O Wise One?"

"It is known to me, honourable one."

"That is well, for if you would receive from me the Four Pearl Thimbles of Chen-tse, then must I have your promise on the sacred toe of Buddha that never shall priest of the temple seek the girl who was lost. If you give not that pledge, O Wise One, never again shall the four missing thimbles lie in the ark in the holy of holies of the Temple of Eternal Purity."

It was plain that the priest was puzzled by Plummer's words, for he did not know that the girl who had escaped was alive. He still believed her to have been drowned, as was reported. But since a girl had no value in China, and he did not know that her gaze had profaned the holy of holies in the temple, he gave the pledge. And looking at Vali Mata-Vali, Sexton Blake at last knew her secret.

"Then let us to business," said Plummer, after a backward glance at the woman. "Here in this case are the Four Thimbles of Chen-tse. Examine them, if it pleases you."

As he spoke he laid a purple velvet case on the table, and with fingers that shook as if with the palsy, the senior priest opened it. The other two pressed close, and as their eyes fell on the four wonderful pearls within the case a simultaneous long-drawn "a-i-e" went up. But Plummer had no reverence and no sentiment in the matter. All he wanted now was the bag of diamonds, and said so.

The priests, recalled to the fact that Hong-Lo-Soo's agent still stood there, turned to him to speak. But Blake was ready, and with a swift motion drew out the bag of diamonds. He dropped it gently to the table, and with a scarce-concealed cry of triumph George Marsden Plummer thrust out both hands to catch it.

In the same moment something flashed dully under the light, and the next instant the tense silence was broken by a sound that has sent a chill to many a heart.

Click!

It was the snapping of the lock of the pair of handcuffs which Sexton Blake slid on to Plummer's wrists at the very moment when his fingers were closing about the bag of diamonds.

A terrible oath broke from the master criminal's lips. He tried to straighten up, but found an iron hand holding the jointure of the two steel bands. Then a well-known voice broke upon his ears. "Plummer, I arrest you for murder!"

"Sexton Blake!"

The words came in a sharp whisper.

"Yes. It's been a long chase, Plummer, but— Here is an inspector from the Surete; you are his prisoner!"

At that moment the door had opened, and now Inspectors Journet and Collet rushed in followed by half a dozen men. Plummer made a wild effort to break away, but Blake's hold was too controlling, and he was still struggling when Journet laid his hands on him. At that Blake released his hold, for his part was done. He was anxious to see what the woman would do in the face of this sudden crisis, and he had not long to wait.

She had sprung to her feet at the first ominous snapping of these manacles, and now she was standing close to the wall, about half-way between the couch where she had been reclining and the door. One hand was against the silken tapestry hanging, as if she were weak and found it necessary to support her limbs. Thus the tableau just after Blake had handed over as prisoner the criminal who had led him a longer chase than most.

Then:

"Come to me!"

It was the voice of Vali Mata-Vali raised in utmost urgency. Scarcely had its ringing echo died away than the room was plunged in profound darkness, and then there came the sounds of oaths and a scuffle.

Both Blake and Tinker guessed what that meant. Together they threw themselves in the direction where they had last seen Plummer, but there was no one there. The sounds seemed now to come from across the room, and with an exclamation of impatience Blake felt his way to the door.

After considerable feeling about he found the light switch. Pressing it, he stood ready to rush; but there was now no need. The two French inspectors stood blinking in the middle of the room. Their men were equally bewildered, and of Plummer or Vali Mata-Vali there was not a sign.

Blake raced to the spot where he had seen the woman leaning against the wall. With one sweep of the arm he dragged down the silken tapestry. There was revealed the outline of a stone door, set in the granite wall. Of handle or means of opening there was no sign.

"Journet! Collet! A secret door! They have gone this way! Out after them. They will try to get away in the car."

The two detectives came to their wits quickly enough. Turning, they made for the main door, followed by their men. Blake paused only long enough to tell the three priests to wait, then he and Tinker followed. But they were too late; Vali Mata-Vali had played a trump card.

If George Marsden Plummer had had any doubts about the calibre of his partner, Vali Mata-Vali, they vanished in those few moments during which she displayed a quickness of thought and an initiative that he himself could not have equalled.

Once he was through the secret door behind the curtains he found himself in a narrow stone passage. They raced along this until they came to a flight of stone steps. At the top she paused.

"Listen!"

Her warning whisper held him motionless. Somewhere in the distance they could hear faint sounds which they knew came from the efforts of Blake and the others to find a way of opening the secret door.

"We can reach the garage at the back by these stairs," she told him. "I didn't think we should need to use this way or I should have told you about it. They will soon be out of the room, and will locate the garage. We must get over the rear drawbridge before they do so.

Give me the bag. We've got the diamonds, at least, but I don't know what we can do about those handcuffs."

Plummer cursed Blake violently.

"Let me get my hands on the driving-wheel, and I'll manage. We can get these confounded things off later. Let's get going."

She clutched the bag of diamonds in her arms and flew down the stairs. Plummer was close at her heels. They reached the bottom, and found another narrow passage.

"This follows the course of one of the inner walls of the chateau, and is actually inside it," she panted as they raced along. "It isn't far now."

The passage turned abruptly at right-angles. They skidded round the corner and reached the end about twenty yards on. Here they were brought to a full stop by another secret door, but when Vali Mata-Vali opened that they found themselves in what Plummer took to be a cellar.

The girl closed the door, and they raced across the cellar to a door which opened into one of the places that had been turned into a garage. Here, ready for the road, was a powerful racing car.

Plummer made a dive for the driving-seat and slid his manacled hands over the wheel. Vali pressed a lever in the wall that swung the big double doors inward. Then Plummer saw a gravelled drive outside that, curving slightly, led to the inner end of the secondary drawbridge, the same which had caught Blake's eye as they approached the place. Blake was to regret that he hadn't followed his first instinct to make sure if that way was guarded as well as the front.

The car was already moving by the time Vali Mata-Vali swung aboard and slid down beside Plummer. By the time it was half-way to the end of the drawbridge the engine was roaring and Plummer was stepping on it hard.

They shot on to the drawbridge like a projectile, and were more than halfway across it, before bullets began peppering the car and spattering the bridge all about them. They could not hear the sound of the guns from which they came.

Then Vali Mata-Vali leant close to Plummer. She had to shout to make him hear.

"Faster! Faster! Look at the end of the bridge. They're raising the draw!"

She was right. Plummer emitted a short, sharp oath, then he

jammed the accelerator flat to the floorboards. The car rocked crazily as the bridge moved beneath them. They were doing close on ninety now, and it wouldn't have needed much to send them somersaulting through the guard chains at the side.

They seemed suddenly to be climbing. The end of the draw was certainly beginning to lift from the piers on which it rested. It looked like certain death to try to cross that rising line that marked the end, but Plummer held the car straight for it.

They thundered on to what seemed certain death. The girl clutched at the side, her eyes fixed tensely on the steadily rising end of the draw. Then the car shot up to the edge and over. For the fraction of a moment water showed beneath them as they roared up in what seemed a certain death leap. For an appreciable time the car was in the air before it struck ground on the other side. It bounded into the air again, while Plummer hung on to the wheel with his manacled hands. It hit the ground again, made one more bound, struck, and skidded into a bush, then as Plummer managed to straighten out, it held the ground and went roaring down the road towards the rear gates of the park.

Astounded at the sheer nerve of the leap, Inspector Collet's men stood gaping. When an angry shout snapped them out of their trance, however, they raced after the car, emptying their weapons as they went.

Back in the main courtyard of the chateau, Sexton Blake and Tinker were just in time to see the car shoot over the rising end of the drawbridge. Blake swore.

"If he keeps on four wheels he'll do it, Tinker!"

"He's done it all right!" shouted Tinker. "Look! There he goes!"

Blake took one look at the vanishing fugitives, then he turned and made for their own car. The police were also rushing for their cars, and within moments the whole fleet was roaring across the main drawbridge, sirens screaming. There was one hope of cutting off the fugitives, and that was to reach the main road before them.

But Plummer knew the slimness of his chances. Furiously angry and more chagrined than he had ever been in his life, he was determined to beat pursuit despite the handicap of manacled wrists.

Vali Mata-Vali didn't utter a sound. She just hung on and left it to Plummer. If they got past the main gates it would be a wild race, and nothing she could do would help just then. Plummer was getting everything possible out of the powerful engine.

They reached the main road, and, a few seconds later, flashed past the main gates of the park. They were open, and, coming towards them, they saw the first of the pursuing cars.

Plummer shouted something she did not hear. They took a sharp corner at such terrific speed that they skidded half round. Miraculously Plummer straightened out again. Just ahead of them was a farm-cart loaded with roots. It seemed impossible that Plummer could get through between it and the bank, but he did it with no more than an inch to spare. They heard only fragments of the frightened driver's angry protests as the wind whipped them away.

They were in a long stretch of straight road where Vali Mata-Vali could look back. Plummer heard her give a cry of joy.

"They've crashed. The first car has struck the farm-cart. It's somersaulting. O-h-h! Splendid! It's in flames, but they are out. The horse is climbing the bank. The cart is matchwood. The other cars can't get past. We've got them! We've got them!"

Plummer grinned—the first time since Sexton Blake had snapped those manacles on his wrists. He dare not look back, but Vali's description was vivid enough for him to picture the scene. He would have given a good many of the diamonds to know that Blake was in the first car.

Vali was still screaming details of as much as she could see when they swept round a bend and the scene of the crash was lost to her.

Plummer didn't want to drive through Paris. He knew of the danger of a telephone message having been sent to the Prefecture as a warning. If they got hemmed inside the city it would be almost impossible for them to escape. He had another plan.

When he came to a branch road that would take them towards Auteuil or south away from the city, he swung south. Vali Mata-Vali knew now what was in his mind. He intended making a detour and coming round again to the north of the city. It would bring them dangerously close to St. Cloud, but Plummer was figuring this was about the last move the police would credit him with. He was right. From the moment he took that turning Plummer was lost to the ken of his pursuers.

They, however, had plenty to think about. It was only by chance that Blake and Tinker were not in the leading car. In the mad rush back in the courtyard of the chateau to take after Plummer by the first means available, each man had rushed to the car which happened to be nearest. Blake and Tinker tumbled over the side of a big police touring car while the driver was already letting in his clutch.

From all sides came the police, foiled, hot and swearing. Inspector Collet happened to be in the car that was first on to the main drawbridge with Blake's car close behind.

They all saw the car bearing the fugitives when it thundered past the gates, and none of their own drivers needed any urging. There was deep chagrin at the way in which, despite his manacles, Plummer had outwitted them.

Had it not been that Plummer was the first to encounter the farm-cart and frighten both driver and horse, there is little doubt that the police cars would have got past safely enough, for they would have slowed down automatically. But hot foot on Plummer as they were, the man was still hauling on the bit and trying to soothe the horse when the roaring procession appeared.

It was too much for the horse. In one wild leap it tried to climb the bank at the side of the road. This swung the heavy cart right across the crown of the road, and a collision was inevitable. The driver of the leading car jammed on the brakes with such urgency that the heavy car skidded violently. The rear wheels struck the bank, hurling it back. It rebounded, and then turned three somersaults, smashing the farm-cart to matchwood as it went.

The driver of the second car had also jammed on his brakes and brought the vehicle to a stop without disaster not six inches from the wreckage of the farm-cart. The horse had dragged clear in the collision and had succeeded in getting over the top of the bank.

But Blake and the others had no time for the horse. They had seen a burst of flame in the road ahead, and with horror in their eyes were rushing to the rescue.

All four occupants of the wrecked car had been thrown clear. Two were lying in huddled postures at one side of the road. It was impossible to tell yet whether they were dead or not. Another was on his knees groping about blindly, and a third, whom Blake recognised as Inspector Collet, was on his feet staggering about like a drunken man. It was a miracle that they had not been trapped in the blazing car. Had it been a saloon they would never have got clear, and would now be in the midst of that holocaust.

Even if it had not been necessary to attend to the injured, the blazing wreck in the middle of the road and the barricade formed by the smashed farm-cart and the great heap of scattered roots would have effectually prevented their continuing the pursuit. Had they known which way Plummer would take, they could have turned and circumvented him at St. Cloud. But it was futile to try and guess, and by the time they were free to continue they knew it would be a sheer waste of time.

It was nearly two hours later when they were able to resume their journey into Paris, and by the time the cars drew up in the courtyard at the Prefecture, Sexton Blake was sunk in black despondency.

It was a bitter, bitter blow.

CHAPTER 14.   The Wit of a Woman.

SEXTON BLAKE and Monsieur Dupuis were dining together in the Prefect's flat at the Surete. The windows, high up in the ancient building on the Ile de la Cite, were wide open to the summer evening, which was still bright and sunny.

From where he sat, Blake could see the graceful, pointed tower of Notre Dame, with the sinking sun tipping its pinnacle with gold and, now lost to the sun, the squat, grey towers that have gazed down upon so much of France's stirring history. A little to the left was the Seine, with its barges and bridges— a picture that he always found soothing and from nowhere so lovely to look upon as from this spot where he now sat.

Monsieur Dupuis was a host of considerable discrimination. He himself was a gourmet, and, from his predecessor, had inherited a chef who did his utmost to pander to this discrimination. The result was a meal fit to pass the most exacting test, and, during its progress, with wine that was as golden as the dying sun, Blake had found a certain consolation for his chagrin.

By mutual accord they had left a discussion of the Plummer affair until the coffee and liqueur were served. It was a tribute to the chef which every true gourmet must pay; a gourmand would not have thought it necessary.

But when cigars were alight Monsieur Dupuis looked through the blue haze at his guest.

"Well, mon ami, shall we discuss the matter which I know is filling your mind?"

"It seems sacrilege to insult such food and wine with something so unpleasant," sighed Blake, "but I suppose it must be done. What a fiasco it has been!"

"You take it too hard. After all, you set out to recover the Pearl Thimbles of Chen-tse and you have succeeded."

"I know—I know, but Plummer has got away with the diamonds, and, more than that, he has done three murders."

"We have no definite proof of that, but I think you are right."

"I am sure of it. Plummer was the person who posed as Henry Dean. It was Plummer who killed Sam Danvers. Danvers will be no loss to society. And it was Plummer, posing as Henry Dean, who did the double killing at Arundel. So you can understand my chagrin, mon ami. Had those murders been done in France you would be feeling exactly the same "

"You are right, mon ami. And I feel the same now. Never fear, we shall soon have word of Plummer. He and Mademoiselle Vali Mata-Vali cannot get many miles in an open car without their passage being seen. Ah, mon ami," he sighed, "there is a one for you—young, beautiful, everything she could desire, Paris at her feet—and she must throw it all away for this 'type,' Plummer."

"It would be interesting to know how they came together," rejoined Blake thoughtfully. "She is all you say, mon ami, but I have a feeling that mademoiselle was a very sophisticated young woman before she ever saw Paris. I have heard a few things. Have you ever been in China?"

"I was in Saigon in our own Indo-China for a few days, that is all."

"I meant farther up the coast—Canton, Shanghai, Peking."

"I regret—no."

"Still you have many temples in your Indo-French colonies, so will understand. I have some reason to believe that Mademoiselle Vali Mata-Vali was, at a very tender age, a temple girl in one of the temples in China. They are a caste peculiar to themselves. At what age or how or why she left there I do not know, but I am certain that she had a very close connection with the Pearls of Chen-tse long before she came to Paris."

"What you say is interesting and, I think, correct."

"No amateur could have acted as she did when I snapped the bracelets on Plummer's wrists. I have never seen a more lightning initiative. And George Marsden Plummer would never have given to any amateur the immediate obedience he gave to her when she cried: 'Come to me!'"

"Parbleu, you are right there. It was a thing of the most remarkable nature. And the way he drove that car!"

"Yes. It isn't the first tight spot Plummer has been in. We shall never be safe in counting on his capture until we have him 'hog-tied,' as they say in America. Just the same, he is badly handicapped while those manacles are on his wrists. They will choose the first possible opportunity to get them off. That means they will stop somewhere as soon as possible—somewhere, I venture to say, where they figure they will be safe for a brief time at least. We've got to get him, mon ami; we've got to get him. And I believe they will stop somewhere between here and the Channel coast."

"I agree with you. But what can we do until we get in reports from my men? They are out in every direction scouring the roads. The police of every town and city and village in France have been warned. The moment a definite clue comes in, we shall be after them. Rest easy, mon ami, they shall not escape us."

Blake did not respond at once. He was thinking. He knew that what the prefect said bore a lot of truth. Nevertheless, he felt uneasy. He remembered how Plummer had wriggled out of other corners as tight as this, and as recently as this very day hadn't he given them the slip—even if the chief credit of that was due to Vali Mata-Vali? At last he looked up.

"Do you know, mon ami, if Mademoiselle Vali Mata-Vali possessed any property other than the chateau at St. Cloud?"

"I do not know, but it is a thing we should be able to find out. Wait for me, please."

He rose and left the room. Blake rose also and walked to one of the open windows where the panorama was more extended than from where he had been sitting. He was still standing there, pondering on the puzzle, when M. Dupuis returned.

"Perhaps things will begin to march now, mon ami," he said briskly. "One report has just come in. A car answering to the description, and with two persons who might be the two we seek, was noticed to the north of St. Cloud about an hour after the escape. This was followed by a second report that a car of the same description was seen between Poissy and Vilennes an hour later. That is all."

"It seems to indicate that the car was heading into Normandy, which would bear out my theory."

"That is certainly one of the roads it would be obliged to take."

"Have you put through the inquiry regarding property owned by Mademoiselle Vali Mata-Vali?"

"Yes, urgently. I have instructed that the information shall be telephoned to me in my private apartments. We can do nothing more for the moment, mon ami. You must let me give you a glass of my old brandy. I shall not tell you how it came into my possession, but I can promise you it is superb."

Blake smiled and turned back to the table. It would take nothing short of a riot to cause Monsieur Dupuis to lose his sang-froid so, he asked himself, should he?

They sat down again, and when Blake sipped the old brandy from its big, bell glass he had to agree that his host had not exaggerated. They lit fresh cigars, and got into an interesting discussion on various aspects of criminology which carried on through the deepening dusk. Then the quiet evening was broken by the sudden ringing of the telephone.

Monsieur Dupuis answered it and talked briefly. Twice, Blake heard him mention Poissy and once he spoke of Vilennes. Then he hung up and strode back to the table. He was brisk enough now in action and speech.

"That was a brainwave of yours, mon ami. We have struck something, I think."

"What is it?"

"Mademoiselle Vali Mata-Vali does own property other than the chateau at St. Cloud. She is the owner of an old house that stands on the bank of the river about midway between Foissy and Vilennes. Is that not an indication that the car seen near those places was the one we seek?"

Blake was already on his feet. He could not restrain a feeling of satisfaction that his shot in the dark had struck a target so soon.

"They have not gone past that house," he rejoined. "But how long they will lie low there we do not know. If they intend to wait until the hue and cry has died down, then they may be there for days. On the other hand; if they feel that all France is too dangerous they may leave this same night. We must catch them before they leave that house."

"We shall do so, we shall do so! I shall have a cordon around the whole district within half an hour. And in the meantime we shall be on our way. This time, mon ami, this time they shall not escape."

Blake smiled agreement with his enthusiasm, but, inwardly, he did not feel anything like so confident. He would be ready to call it a day when he actually had his hands on Plummer.

His caution was to prove well inspired.

.   .   .   .

Plummer and Vali Mata-Vali sat together in a large, stone-flagged room that was curtained and furnished after the fashion of the sixteenth century.

The furniture was fine old stuff that would have brought a fancy price at any sale at the Hotel Drouet, although the tapestry was faded

126

and worn. The curtains, too, were faded, and there was a faint, musty odour which is peculiar to old rooms and ancient furniture.

The only lighting was from candles set in several branched silver candlesticks, and although the night outside was warm a log fire burned in the ample fireplace.

They had dined. An old manservant had removed the things, but a carafe of brandy and another of water still remained. From each of these, Plummer was helping himself generously. The girl drank more sparingly and looked a little askance at his copious draughts.

"I'd go easy on that stuff," she warned him with a smile. "If we have to get away to-night you'll need all your wits about you."

Plummer grinned.

"Don't you worry about me, cherie. I can look after myself with this stuff. It wasn't because I had had too much to drink that I was caught back at the chateau. But I'm saying that I couldn't have got out of that jam if it hadn't been for you."

She waved a hand, dismissing her share in the escape. Women are like that when their affections are engaged.

"Poof, that was nothing! I just happened to know about the secret door— and no one could have driven as you did with those things on your wrists."

Plummer flushed with anger as he looked at his wrists which were still red where they had been bruised in removing the manacles. It wasn't anger at her—it was directed towards Sexton Blake.

"I've got a few accounts to settle over this affair, and I'll pay them before I finish," he snarled. "If I'd known you had this place tucked away down here I'd never have gone to the chateau. It was too dangerous. But they won't find us here or get those," and, as he finished speaking, he glanced towards the velvet bag of diamonds which stood on the table for the simple reason that he hadn't been able to let it out of his sight. He was still remembering too vividly how nearly he had lost it at the chateau.

"Shall we have a look at them?" he asked her.

She shrugged.

"If you like. The thing that interests me more is to know how we are to dispose of them."

Plummer laughed easily.

"That's the least of our worries. There's nothing 'hot' about those stones. They're ours just the same as if we had bought them and paid good money for them. If it wasn't for the other"—she knew he referred to the killings he had done over in England— "I'd cock a snook at Sexton Blake. He wouldn't have a single thing on me. And if he tried to pull any stuff about that fool, Fu Won Chang, you know enough about him to settle that. No, cherie, the treasure of the Forty Moons is ours and we're going to cash in on it."

"And after that?" she asked softly. "We've got the whole world to play in, m' dear."

He saw her lift her head as though she were listening. He had heard nothing.

"What is it?"

"I thought I heard a bell ringing. It sounded like the one at the garden door. You can only hear it faintly here. Listen!"

They sat very quiet, listening. For a few moments they heard nothing but a light crackling of the flames and a thinner sound which they knew to be the river washing against the stone foundations of the house.

Then, from what seemed a great distance, there came the shrilling of a bell. Vali Mata-Vali rose cautiously.

"I'll go and see what it is," she whispered. "There's only old Pierre and he's partially deaf."

"I'll come, too," growled Plummer.

He got to his feet and drew out his gun.

"If anyone tries to pull any stuff here to-night, believe me, they'll take a slug," he told her.

"It can't be the police. It must be someone local who has seen lights in this room. Better stay here."

"I'm coming."

She made no further protest but walked quietly to the door with Plummer close behind. Opening the door she stepped into a bleak passage, which extended in both directions. She paused here and they stood again listening.

Once more the sound of the bell reached them, this time more distinctly and sounding urgent. Vali Mata-Vali started along the passage quickly. Plummer kept at her heels.

Some distance down, she turned into a branch passage on the right and, again, a little distance along that, turned to the left. Now they could hear the bell clearly, it stopped suddenly and then voices came to them, one very loud, as though trying to overcome the deafness of another person.

Vali Mata-Vali began to run. Plummer followed suit. They came to another turn in the passage and, at this corner, the girl stopped so abruptly that Plummer almost fell over her. Then the girl's voice rose in a startled scream.

"Back, back! It's the police. Come with me."

But Plummer didn't obey. He pushed her aside and peered along the passage. He saw the manservant, Pierre, being thrust aside while men pushed through the doorway. With a savage curse, he threw up his gun and began to shoot.

It didn't matter to him which one of the oncoming mob he hit. One was as good as another.

The girl tried to drag him back.

"Oh, come, come," she kept urging. "There is one way out if we are in time."

Plummer obeyed, not because she pleaded but because he had just remembered that he had left the bag of diamonds back in the salon.

He whirled round and caught her hand, dragging her along with him at top speed. She must have remembered the diamonds, too, for her feet flew after his.

Turning after turning they took until they were in sight of the salon door. Light flowed out from the room and they thought they could make it. But from the gloom of the passage beyond that half-open door came a shout,

"Halt! We've got you covered."

Plummer knew now that he would never reach that door alive. He drew up and prepared to shoot it out, but the girl was talking in urgent tones.

"Come, come back this way. There is the way I told you about. We can make it."

He turned and they sped back the way they had come. Guns racketed behind them and bullets spattered against the stone. But they were quickly round a corner and then the girl dragged him into a side passage, much narrower than the others.

They sped along this and Vali Mata-Vali guided him down a flight of narrow stone stairs into a damp cellar. Plummer found matches and she showed him a big, oaken door that was barred. He threw off the bar and dragged the doer open.

Above them they could hear shouts and excited questions. He swore and almost turned back as he recognised the voice of Sexton Blake dominating the others—but the girl dragged him on until he found himself standing beside a small motor launch that was moored cunningly behind a wooden gate in the foundation wall of the house. He knew what was needed now.

He sprang to the gate and dragged it open. Vali Mata-Vali was already in the boat when he tumbled over the side. He pressed the self-starter and pushed in the clutch. The boat was gathering speed by the time they were out from under the house and turning.

He didn't know the river in that part and he didn't know what obstacles he might encounter. But that didn't matter. Nothing mattered now.

He cursed again, then he opened the throttle and, with a racketing like that of a machine-gun, they roared off into the night.

. .   .   .   .

Sexton Blake heard that departure and, although he couldn't see the fugitives, he knew well enough what it meant.

He was filled with bitter anger. It was enough to make the saints weep. He had actually laid his arch enemy by the heels twice in one day, had had the bracelets on his wrists once and now he was gone. Once, it had been by the quick wit of a woman. Was this second escape due to the same quick wit?

It was little consolation to him that he had recovered the Pearl Thimbles of Chen-tse. It seemed to matter not at all when he found the treasure of the Forty Moons intact on the table in the salon. Nor did he find much satisfaction when, two days later, he walked into Hong-Lo-Soo's private apartments in the premises in Packer's Court and handed him the precious pearls that had been the cause of the whole business. If there was to be any consolation at all, he found it in the pathetic gratitude of Fu Won Chang who, when Blake had explained matters, was taken under the personal care of Hong-Lo-Soo.

For Sexton Blake knew that not only was George Marsden Plummer back in circulation again but he realised that he now had the asset of a beautiful and quick-witted partner.

Hong-Lo-Soo, however, insisted in his wise old way that there was far, far more to bring him satisfaction in knowing that he had snatched back a soul from terrible wanderings in the outer darkness to the regions of light and sanity.

And, looking at Fu Won Chang, Blake conceded that, perhaps, he was right.

THE END.
[53000 WORDS]